A Chance For More

Zanne Sweeney

DEDICATION

There are people in my life who continue to encourage and inspire me to write. I loving dedicate *A Chance For More* to you. Lori, Mom, Kaleigh, and Caitlin, a special thank you for your edits and thumbs up. To all of you who read my first book, *Neighbors* and asked for the sequel. Here it is! Finally, to my husband, Mark, who lovingly jokes he is a book widower. Honey, you know you love it when I'm writing; that gives you sole control of the clicker. Thank you, this one's for you!

Authors note: *A Chance For More* can be read as a stand alone; however I recommend that you read my inaugural book, *Neighbors* first. The stories do connect and there is a spoiler in *A Chance For More* if you have not read *Neighbors* yet. Enjoy!

Amazon
http://www.amazon.com/Neighbors/dp/B00H9TED3U

BarnesandNoble
http://www.barnesandnoble.com/c/zanne-sweeney

iTunes
https://itunes.apple.com/us/book/neighbors/id781766803?mt=11

GooglePlay
http://books.google.com/books?printsec=frontcover&id=MdJTAgAAQBAJ#v=onepage&q&f=false

ACKNOWLEDGMENTS

Thank you M.C.
Pikoso.kz/Shutterstock

This book is intended for mature readers. It is a work of fiction

Chapter 1

Shelby snuggled deeper under her down covers reminiscing about the Christmas Day she had just spent with her Mom. She, her sister Sara and Sara's fiancé, Danny had traveled to Wyoming to spend their Christmas vacation with her Mom, Grace. Her Mom had recently moved to Landgrove, Wyoming and this was their first visit to her new home. The day had been fun, festive, and enlightening. Shelby knew that her Mom's new neighbors had everything to do with how well the day had gone.

After a Christmas dinner feast with just the four of them, her Moms' neighbors had come over for dessert; Betty, who was her Mom's new friend and Betty's husband Josh. Josh's brother Jed, a strikingly handsome man who couldn't keep his eyes off her Mom, and Clay, Jed's son, an unbelievably gorgeous man who literally took Shelby's breath away.

Jed had brought her Mom a pregnant cat for a Christmas present, which her Mom had been delighted with. Shelby thought that the gesture of adding to her Mom's small ranch was incredibly sweet. Her mom loved animals and now, since she had moved to the ranch from her long time home in New Jersey, it afforded her the opportunity to have them, lots of them. Shelby also grasped the significance of the handsome rancher giving her Mom a pet. In Shelby's book if a man gave a woman a pet he was indicating he was ready for a committed relationship.

The group of eight had enjoyed dessert and coffee, played Wii and exchanged presents. Shelby also couldn't help but notice that her Mom and Jed had casually been touchy feely the entire day, Shelby didn't think they even knew they were touching each other, they were just naturally drawn to each other. The energy between the two of them seriously sizzled. During the evening they had heard cars pulling into her Mom's driveway, and when the unknown visitors rang the bell Jed protectively and gently had tucked her Mom behind him as he answered the door. Shelby shivered thinking how that had been such a protective gesture that it was sexy hot. The visitors turned out to be more of her Mom's new friends. They came bearing gifts; two sheep to replace the sheep that had been poisoned a few months earlier. The tragedy was still a mystery. No one could figure out who would do such a mean thing, and why to her Mom's sheep. The sheriff was still investigating.

Through out the day Clay had been attentive to Shelby. He sat next to her when he could, and when she snuck peeks at him he always seemed to be already looking at her, staring actually. They had engaged in a lively debate on who would win the BCS Bowl. Shelby was knowledgeable regarding football, much to Clays delight. She knew her football and she enjoyed that Clay spoke with her candidly about the game. Most men poo-pooed women when they spoke about football. Not Clay, he wasn't patronizing or condescending.

At the end of the evening Shelby had helped Clay put the new sheep in the barn and they also checked on her mom's new barn cat. Shelby tried to get Clay to give her some insight regarding their parents but Clay said it was her Mom's story to tell.

"Clay" Shelby said exasperated that he wouldn't spill his guts. "He gave her a cat, for gosh sakes."

"Yup, that does scream commitment doesn't it?" Clay laughed.

"Really you're not going to tell me anything?"

"Shelby they're happy, both of them. I'll tell you this, when I find the person that makes me want forever I'll be giving her a pet too. It's like practice for having children. Maybe it's a Wyoming thing." He teased.

Shelby sighed. "No, you're right. I know girls that have gotten pets as presents from their boyfriends. I'd always thought it was an affectionate overture."

"Has anyone ever given you one?" Clay asked anxious to hear her answer.

"Nope, I never got to that juncture in a relationship." She answered laughing, but Clay could see sadness dusting her beautiful blue eyes.

"Why's that? Seems to me you'd have men waiting in line to claim you."

"That's sweet of you to say. I guess I'm too picky," she wavered then continued. "I tend to like guys who are loyal and I think those kind of men are all but extinct." Shelby laughed at her analogy.

"Well darling, you just haven't been dating in the right state." Clay had joked back, but just the way he said it made Shelby think he wasn't joking at all.

As they talked Shelby watched him move with deftness for such a big man. He lifted the heavy grain sacks that had been a present for her mom from his Uncle and Aunt, with ease. His leg muscles pulling the fabric of his jeans taunt over his powerful thighs and backside when he squatted. He had broad shoulders and he was tall, so much taller than her 5'5" frame. Shelby loved how his thick raven colored hair would fall teasingly across his brow and that he'd unconsciously push it back with his fingers. His eyes were hazel; a beautiful green that with little brown flecks that could hypnotize an unsuspecting female. Not her of course, she had been down that route with men and she knew a player when she saw one, no matter what state she was in.

Shelby did enjoy talking to him though. She found him to be smart and he had a great sense of humor. She discovered throughout the evening that he had played football in college, at State, where his father still coached. He also co owned the cattle ranch that bordered two sides of her Mom's property with his father. Clay was beyond handsome and Shelby knew that usually meant gay or trouble with a capital T. She thought perhaps he had been attentive to her because she was 'fresh meat', so to speak. They were in a small town and God knew how many young women there were in the area. Maybe Clay had already plowed through them all and needed a new diversion. Whatever the case, Shelby knew she needed to steer clear. There were two problems with that, first was that she had thoroughly liked being with him. They had struck up a camaraderie that would suggest to anyone not knowing them that they known each other for longer than a few hours. Secondly, she didn't want to put herself in an awkward situation with her Mom's new neighbors. The problem was that she and her sister and Danny were going to spend tomorrow afternoon and evening with him at a big day after Christmas party. Clay had invited them and it really did sound fun, skating, ice hockey games, coed football, snow mobile rides, food, drink, and dancing. The party was to be held on one of Clays friend's ranches. Shelby fell asleep thinking about the charming young cowboy. She realized that steering clear of him was going to be a challenge.

The next morning Shelby helped her Mom feed her growing menagerie. So far she had two sheep, four egg laying hens, a rooster, that crowed too damn early in the morning, two frisky puppies, and now the pregnant cat. When her Mom's Uncle had passed away he left his small spread to her. She had packed up her life in New Jersey and headed west. There hadn't been anything to keep her in Jersey, except perhaps memories. Shelby's dad had passed some time ago. Although she and Sara were still in Jersey, they were living their own lives. Neither begrudged their Mom a chance to restart her life, even if it was clear across the United States.

Clay arrived right on time to take them to the party. They packed up the bed of his truck with all the items Clay had told them they might need. Along with what Clay had recommended they bring, the girls also packed the truck with a ton of food. 'Never arrive empty handed, their Mom had taught them. Chicken wings, a crabmeat dip, a large chip and cheese salad, and home made baked goods were safely stored into Tupperware and tucked into the jam packed truck bed. Clay had brought a cooler full of drinks, ice hockey equipment for Danny, and a grill. They waved goodbye to their Mom and headed off.

The drive took 30 minutes but the time passed quickly with the friendly conversation and the pretty mountain scenery that surrounded them. Shelby couldn't help but feel humbled by the beautiful Wyoming landscape. The truck turned and twisted down one dirt road and then another before arriving at a private driveway that was distinguished with prominent stone pillars holding up an arched sign with - HAVEN, cut into it. Clay drove his truck right up to an enormous barn so they could unload and then he left to park in a field along with the other cars. The barn was huge and had obviously been cleared to accommodate the party. Bales of hay were placed around the edges for sitting. A little platform was off to the side and Shelby could see that a band was setting up. A long table was beginning to accumulate dishes and platters of food. Outside the large sliding barn door grills were set up side by side, and in another area coolers and kegs were corralled in a small pen creating a makeshift bar.

Clay took them first to meet the host, his friend Gus. Gus welcomed them and gave Shelby the once over which prompted Clay to place his hand possessively on Shelby's shoulder. Shelby gave Clay a little 'what's up with that?' look and Clay simply smiled and continued giving them the tour of the ranch turned party grounds. Everywhere they went people stopped to talk to Clay. The guys shook his hand or slapped his shoulder as good friends do. The girls unabashedly eyed him like he was piece of good chocolate. Some more brazen females went out of their way to fleetingly touch him, leaving no doubt what they wanted. Clay efficiently, without hurting feelings always shook loose as he stood next to Shelby

The four of them walked down to a pond that had been cleared of snow. Part of the pond was set up for ice hockey and another small portion for regular skating. A group of guys and girls were hovering near a bon fire and that's where Clay headed. He cordially introduced them to everyone and told the men that Danny wanted to join the ice hockey games. The guy's who were forming teams quickly welcomed Danny, and Sara was just as quickly ensconced with the girlfriend group.

Satisfied that they were settled Clay walked Shelby back towards the barn.

"So what's with the hand on the shoulder stuff?" Shelby asked Clay.

"I just thought it be better for the guys to think you were with me."

Shelby grunted out a laugh. "Seriously, you did not just say that."

"If these Neanderthals think you're available they will be all over you." His answer hinted of a tease, but his eyes were dead serious.

"I am available Clay." Shelby huffed.

"I don't want you to be available to them, just me." He shot back too confidently.

Shelby took a second to gather some emotional control.

"Mmmm... You're kind of pissing me off right now. Do you get that?"

"Yea, I figured. Listen, I just want to get to

know you better and I don't want every single guy here to be competing with me. I thought if I sort of put out signals you were with me I could keep you to myself at least for a little while."

Shelby considered what he had just said. She gave him points for honesty.

"Thanks, I think. I'd like to get to know you better also, but Clay I'm only here for a week. I'm not looking for anything, you know… a relationship, and I don't do one - night stands." Shelby stopped walking forcing him to turn and face her. "I enjoy talking with you Clay, I do. Besides, what if pretending to be with you here, now, I miss out on meeting my Mr. Right?" Shelby teased him with a poke in the ribs with her elbow.

Clay grabbed her around the waist and brought her snuggly into his chest, the top of her head not even reaching his chin.

"What if I'm Mr. Right?" He teased back as

he held her loosely around her waist and looked down into her twinkling blue eyes. They both started laughing relishing the ease in which they could banter with each other.

The coed football tournament, that Clay had told Shelby about the day before and both were excited to participate in, was being held in a large hay field. Clay had told Shelby that they played a round robin format. Twenty - five minute games with a minute half time to change sides of the field. Seven people to a team and there had to be a girl on the field. Winners of the football tourney got to take first showers, something that Shelby realized was a coveted prize since the field usually turned to mud and the hot water usually ran out on the losing teams.

Shelby wore yoga pants, a turtleneck, a Giants jersey, Manning, of course, hiking boots, and a knit cap. Her blond hair poked out from underneath it and Clay had to stop himself from reaching out to tuck the errant hairs from her rosy cheeks. Shelby was beautiful. She had brilliant blue eyes, a smattering of freckles on her nose. Her skin was clear and she wasn't plastered with make up like other girls. She was a tiny, curvaceous woman. Her breasts were full and her hips flared perfectly showcasing her flat stomach. Clay knew that Shelby was an athlete. She had played lacrosse in college. The football enthusiasts gathered around bales of hay forming an on deck team area, near a second bon fire, to work out the teams.

Clay and Shelby were on the same team along with his good friend, Ricky. The players rotated positions through out the games. The guys on Shelby's team began to appreciate the fact that Shelby could actually play. She caught passes, set blocks, and she could throw a spiral. Shelby noticed that most of other girls playing were giggling 'hubby hunters,' as she called them. They would fall just so a guy would pick them up. She guessed their tactics worked because most of them seemed to find a guy to dote on them.

Clay and Shelby's team made it to the final round. Their opponents team consisted of a guy named Lars, who was a mountain of a man, who Shelby learned had played for Oregon, a couple other big guys, and a girl that could hold her own with the guys, her name was Liz, she was 5'8" and built. She wasn't a frilly little 'hubby hunter', the girl could kick ass. She also couldn't keep her eyes off of Lars, who Shelby thought was a bit of an egotistical jerk.

The championship game was tied. The field was now almost completely mud and cold slush. The players were becoming more competitive but in a friendly way. Shelby and Liz had been battling throughout the game. Shelby may have been smaller than Liz but she held her own and her quickness was an asset she had been utilizing. Lars had helped Shelby off the ground a few times and then smacked her ass his hand lingering a little too long, which Shelby didn't appreciate, and from the looks of it neither did Liz. Shelby had once again slipped in the mud and gone done after setting a block and once again Lars was right there to assist her up. This time Shelby refused his hand but when she stood on her own he still gave her ass a smack. Shelby turned and glared at him.

"You cave man, you touch my ass one more time and you'll be eating your testicles."

"Whoa, kitten has claws." Lars said holding his hands up giving her a Cheshire cat grin.

"Lars knock- it off." Said Ricky who had seen what had been happening.

"You going to do something about it?" Lars intimidated.

"Asshole." Shelby said as she grabbed Ricky's arm and led him back to the group.

"What's with that jerk?" Shelby asked.

He thinks he's God's gift to women. They usually line up for him. He's not use to someone not tripping over themselves to be with him." Ricky informed her as they made their way back to the huddle.

Clay noticed the slight frown on Shelby's face the second she entered the huddle.

His eyes found hers. "What's the matter?"

"Nothing." she bit out. "Lets beat these guys." Clay looked away from Shelby a prickle of concern shot through him. He glanced over Shelby's head shooting a questioning look at Ricky who just shrugged his shoulders. Ricky wasn't going to open his mouth. Clay wouldn't like how Lars had been touching Shelby. He'd always been down field and he hadn't seen what Lars had been doing. Ricky wasn't sure what the deal was between Clay and Shelby, but he'd known his friend long enough to recognize when Clay liked someone. He definitely liked Shelby, the small touches, little smiles, the fact that he'd watch Clay pass up a sure fuck; Rick would have to ask him later.

Clay was quarterbacking the play and the score was tied. A crowd had assembled near the bon fire. The rest of the party had heard the final game was a barn - burner and they wanted to watch. Both teams knew there was only enough time for two more plays. Clay dropped back to pass and was scrambling, Lars was pursuing him in a big time rush. Shelby was darting down the field with Liz right next to her. Shelby made a quick v cut towards the sideline and Clay recognized the move from one she'd made before, he threw the ball towards her. The pass was sailing slightly away but Shelby leapt up, batted it up before she acrobatically managed to haul it in. The fans were roaring their approval as she scampered down the muddy sideline towards the end line when she was suddenly and violently upended. Shelby went down hard sliding out of bounds with a winded Liz landing on top of her.

Shelby was on her back holding the ball and Liz lay across her on her stomach.

"Shit." Shelby grunted out once she got her breath back.

"Shit." Said Liz gasping for air. Neither girl moved.

They looked at each other and burst out laughing. Shelby noticed then how very pretty Liz was. Straight white teeth, gorgeous chocolate brown eyes pink cheeks, smooth brown hair.

"Great tackle." Said Shelby.

"Fucking great catch." Said Liz.

The girls could hear the guys as they ran towards them. They were both a little out of breath so they helped each other up.

"So... You and Clay, huh?" Liz asked candidly.

"No, we're friends. He's my Mom's neighbor."

"Really, I wish someone would look at me the way he looks at you."

Shelby cocked her head at Liz giving her a knowing smile. "Like Lars?"

"Yea, like Lars, pretty obvious, right?"

"A little."

They started to walk towards their respective huddles.

"Wish I knew how to get him to look at me the way Clay looks at you."

"You know Liz, my Mom always told me if you really like something set it free. If it comes back to you it's yours forever, if it doesn't, it was never yours to begin with."

"Sooooo pretend I don't like him?"

"Well if he's use to you, or girls in general, always chasing him, maybe he needs to be reminded how special you are."

"Is that how you got Clay?"

"I don't have Clay, we're friends." Shelby huffed sending her a smile.

"Ha, keep telling yourself that friend." Liz clapped Shelby on the back and sent her off to her own huddle laughing. The men on their teams reached them and offered them well earned pats on the back, Shelby for her great catch and Liz for saving the touchdown with her great tackle.

Back in the huddle Shelby's team knew they only had one more chance to score.

"It's Shelby's turn to QB." Ricky said.

The huddle got quiet.

"It's okay I don't have to." Shelby said recognizing the seriousness of the situation, even though it was a fun, coed football game being played in a plowed hay field.

"No, you should," said Clay. "They don't know how good an arm Shelby has." Clay spoke to his team. "I think we all go deep and let Shelby air it out."

"Shelby can you throw 30 yards?" One of the other guys asked.

"I sure as heck will try." She answered

honestly.

They broke huddle and Shelby saw that Lars was in the rusher position. Liz gave Shelby a little shrug of her shoulders as if to say 'she had no idea why he was lined up there.' Shelby called for the ball to be hiked and dropped back to pass. She knew she needed to give the team time to get down field so she started to scramble to her right. Lars was running full speed towards her. He was like a tank bearing down on her; she ducked under one of his beefy arms as she tried to stay on her feet while avoiding the imposing man hell bent to bring her down. Shelby saw that Clay had a step on the man covering him so she used every bit of strength she had as she launched the ball into the air hoping it would reach him. As the ball left her hand she was viciously slammed into the ground by Lars, her back hit the frozen sloppy ground and jarred the air from her lungs. She heard cheering but she had no idea which team was doing the cheering, all she knew was that asshole Lars had laid a big time hit on her that would have been flagged in the Pro's. Lars lay on top of her, his head above her head, his hips over hers.

"How's it feel to have a real man on top of you?" he whispered in her ear.

Shelby's lungs burned from lack of oxygen and the air to ground take down had her head ringing like church bells. She couldn't move her arms that were pinned under Lars large frame, but she could move her one leg. With no air coming into her battered body she used every determined cell she could muster as she brought her knee up sharply solidly connecting with Lars balls. He grunted in pain at the unforeseen impact and slowly rolled off her to lie on his side cupping his privates. Shelby moved to lie on her side away from him. With his imposing weight off of her she fought for the air her body was clamoring for. Downfield both teams saw that their teammates where still on the ground, and neither of them were moving. The celebrating and congratulatory high fives halted as they quickly ran back to them.

Liz reached them first; she knelt between Lars and Shelby with her back to Lars.

"Shelby, Oh my gosh, Shelby are you okay?" She rubbed Shelby's back clearly concerned. Lars had gotten into a sitting position still cupping his nads. Liz turned to him and glared.

"You fucking asshole! Are you nuts! What is your problem?" Lars paled and looked positively sick that Liz was yelling at him.

Clay reached them next, still clutching the game ball he knelt near Shelby, his face belayed how alarmed he was, his hand was gently gripping her hip. "Shel's, what happened? You okay?"

"I'll tell you what happened." Liz spit out. "Big bad ass Oregon State rusher decided it would be hard for her to throw over him so he wanted to rush. He couldn't stop the pass so Mr. Competitive here slammed her into the ground."

Clay went to stand up. His jaw was tense and Shelby felt the tension coursing through him. He was going to kick Lars ass, or at least try. Lars was huge. Shelby didn't want a fight. She grabbed Clay by the arm sleeve.

"Clay." she managed to wheeze out.

Her hand reaching out to him froze Clay in his tracks. She was so tiny. A surge of protectiveness welled up within him and he moved towards her letting her know he wouldn't leave her. Clay was enraged and the only thing holding him back from going after Lars was being tethered to Shelby. When Clay saw Shelby struggling to get up he carefully lifted her to her wobbly feet, while keeping his arm around her waist, holding her securely to his strong body. Shelby noticed no one was going anywhere nears Lars who had gotten to his feet and gingerly shuffled away. Her team and even the other team surrounded her to make sure she wasn't injured.

"Did you catch it?" She finally asked once she got her breath back.

Everyone started laughing now they knew she was all right.

"Hell yea he caught it." Ricky yelled with a fist pump in the air. "We won!"

The two teams shook hands with each other, all except Lars that is.

The teams walked back towards the barn caught up in the excitement of the games. Liz remained at Shelby's side, as did Clay. Liz wound her arm around Shelby and gave her a slight squeeze. "That was a great pass Shelby, I'm sorry Lars hit you so hard. I actually don't think he meant to. He doesn't really know his own strength. I'm not apologizing for him, I'm so pissed at him it's not funny."

"What's the deal with you guys anyway?"

Shelby asked.

Liz looked up shyly at Clay and he took the hint and excused himself, telling the two girls he would return with beers. Shelby watched him leave and felt a small void with him no longer holding her. The girls settled on a bale of hay.

"Lars is my older brothers best friend. He has been in my life for as long as I can remember. When we were younger I tagged along with him and my brother everywhere. I guess I was a bit of a tom boy."

"Has he ever, you know, made a move on you?"

"One time, a couple years ago, I really think he was going to, but then my brother walked in to the bar and he moved away."

"Yea, that could be tricky. You don't want to come between best friends."

"Tell me about it. It's just; well I think I've loved Lars forever. We have so much in common. When he's not being Mr. Oregon State he is really a great guy. I hate seeing other girls throw themselves at him."

"Yea that would suck." Nodded her agreement.

"What do you think I should do?"

Shelby was quiet for a second. She didn't know Liz well and she didn't know the situation.

"I don't want to sound mean, but have you asked your other girls friends, or even your Mom? I don't really know you or Lars and I don't want to give advice that would hurt anyone." Shelby told her gently.

"I don't have many girlfriends around here, I was always too tom boyish and my Mom died when I was young so I guess that's a no." Liz answered sadly.

"Well shit, Liz, I'm sorry. Well I won't be here too long but you got a friend here."

Liz smiled and gave Shelby's hand a squeeze.

Clay came back with solo cups filled with beer and they sat drinking with the football players laughing and recapping funny plays from the games. Shelby noticed Lars across the barn standing with his massive arms crossed over his wide chest. As imposing as he looked Shelby noted he also looked a little lost. She also noticed he was watching Liz with almost a forlorn look. There was another guy standing to his right. Shelby assumed it was Liz's brother because they looked so much alike. A small herd of girls were surrounding them, giggling and flirting. Shelby saw that Lars wasn't paying attention to them, much to the girls chagrin.

"Well winners." said Ricky. "I think it's shower time!" Shelby and Clays team all stood to collect their fresh clothes and towels from where they had left them. Clay leaned in to Shelby and said he'd walk her to her shower. The girls got to use the nice one in the ranch office in the upper loft. The guys used the ranch hands communal shower in the ranch hands house.

'That's okay Clay, I'll bring Liz with me, she can show me."

Ricky looked between the two women. "Um, you girls gunna shower together, cause I'd friggin pay to see that?"

Liz looked embarrassed but Shelby didn't miss a beat.

"Sorry Ricky you'll just have to use your imagination of Liz and I all sudsy, washing each others backs in that warm...steamy...small...shower." Shelby let each word slide seductively off her tongue. She grabbed Liz's arm and shot Clay a wink as she led her away. She heard Rick say. "Well shit." Then she heard Clay say to Rick, "Don't even think about it." as the group laughed.

Chapter 2

Shelby and Liz gathered their clothes and headed up stairs.

"Umm Shelby?" Liz hedged nervously. "We aren't really showering together right?"

"No," Shelby laughed. "Sweetie we just need to keep those men on their toes with a little imagery."

Liz smiled and said, "Phew, wasn't sure… you know you being from Jersey and all." Shelby laughed so loud she almost choked.

They took turns in the shower and shared tidbits of information about each other as new friends often do. Liz told Shelby about how she played volleyball at State and explained that because she didn't have a Mom her Dad and brother were a bit protective. She went on to say how they wouldn't even let her buy certain clothes. Shelby liked Liz; she was a small town girl with a big heart. They finished dressing and Shelby helped Liz apply some make up since Liz didn't have any.

"Wow, it's amazing what a little mascara did for your eyes, Liz."

"Really, let me see." Liz looked in the mirror and was shocked at the difference a little mascara made.

Shelby told her. " You're so pretty Liz you don't really need anything more than mascara, and a hint of gloss."

"Shelby, thank you. Do you think Lars will notice?"

"I do and I think others might too."

"Really?"

"Yup, really. So are you ready for my advice? I rarely give any so please don't get mad if it backfires and for the record, I don't like playing games with guys, someone always end up getting hurt. I am usually very honest with them about how I feel. That being said, I think you should avoid Lars a little. Let him come to you. Don't be mean, or coy but simply have a good time without him and not near him. Don't actively try to make him jealous just let him see what he's missing. Also if you are with another guy make sure they know the score. You don't want to lead anyone on. Does that make sense?"

"Yes, perfectly, I'll try to act natural, but it's hard when all I want is to just be with him."

"Liz before we came up here he was watching you, intently, I might add. Ricky told me he could have any women he wanted, do you think that's true?"

"Yes, unfortunately."

"Here's the thing. He doesn't. He doesn't have a girl friend. I don't think he wants another woman. I think he wants you, but has mixed feelings."

"How do you figure?" They had gathered their clothes and were now headed back down to the party.

"Forever he's been your brothers best friend. You grew up with him. Maybe he has to figure out his feelings for you aren't brotherly, or friend like. My point is let him go. Like my Mom's saying I told you earlier. If you release him and he finally realizes what his true feelings are I bet he comes running."

"What if he doesn't?"

"Then sweetie it's time to cut line."

"Shelby you are full of funny sayings! Thanks, and I'll give it a try."

"Just one thing Liz, if he does come around don't play any mind games. Be honest with him, ok?"

"Sure, no problem, and for the record, you

need to be honest with yourself too."

"What do you mean?"

"Clay, darling, you two have so much sexual energy buzzing around you I'd be afraid to light a match."

"Ha, now who has the one liners!" Shelby laughed.

The girls put their dirty clothes away in their respective areas and met back at the make shift bar. The guys were already back from showering and Ricky gave the girls an approving wolf whistle. Clay moved over on his bale of hay to make room for Shelby and Liz sat on a bale of hay next to them.

Ricky went to get them beers and when he returned he joined Liz on her seat of hay. Shelby looked around the barn to find Lars now standing alone. He still hadn't showered. His eyes met hers and he grimaced. She saw him look at Liz and a sad smile took over his face. Shelby almost felt sorry for the big oaf.

"Girls, can we interest you in a snow mobile ride after we finish our beers?" Ricky said.

"I'd love that." Shelby said. "I've never been on one."

"That be fun Liz agreed."

They finished their beers and Shelby and Liz ran to grab their heavy coats. Ricky and Clay pulled the snowmobiles up to the side of the barn and Liz climbed on behind Ricky and Shelby behind Clay. Shelby noticed Lars had followed them out side but had kept his distance. She also noted how he kept clenching and unclenching his fist. She really didn't want to get into the middle of any testosterone induced stuff so once they were speeding down a snow packed path she told Clay what Liz had told her and what she had said to Liz. Clay nodded that he understood.

Clay gave a hand signal to Ricky and

Clay veered their snowmobile off to the left to follow a different trail. The sweet Wyoming air was whipping Shelby's hair that wasn't tucked under her cap. The ride was exhilarating. Shelby loved being outdoors and holding onto the sweet, handsome man in front of her, as they sped down beautiful trails bordered with tall white aspen's felt almost surreal. Clay swung the snowmobile into a little opening on the trail that was shrouded with the gorgeous white barked trees creating a private like setting.

Clay got off the snowmobile and got on again behind Shelby. He put his arms around her waist and pulled her back so she could lean back against him. Against her sensible Shelby better judgment she rested her head back against his muscled chest. Clay was relieved when she relaxed against him; he thought she'd fight the closeness. He really liked holding her.

He was thinking back to her lofting that final pass. It was a perfectly placed spiral.

Not many girls could even throw a spiral much less place it 30 yards downfield. His friends were smitten. Back at the make shift bar one of the guys had kidded him about how he got all the good ones, referring to girls. He saw Shelby tense at the words. He could have smacked his friend. He was so comfortable with her. She fit in great with his friends, she liked sports, she played sports, and she was kind and had already made a friend with one of the shyest girls he knew. Clays heart did a little thud - thud in his chest and he wrapped his arms around Shelby to pull her even closer. He avoided pulling her back into his crotch because he was sporting major wood and he didn't want to scare her off.

"Shelby, I think it's nice you've made friends with Liz. She hasn't had an easy life. Her Mom died when she was small and her Pop is a bit over the top protective."

"She told me that."

"She really likes Lars?"

"Yea, a lot, she has for a really long time."

"I better make sure Ricky doesn't do anything stupid. Larry, her brother and Lars would castrate him."

"That's why I wanted you to know. I don't want there to be any trouble."

"You are a smart girl Shelby Jensen."

Clay kissed the back of her neck and Shelby wiggled away.

"Clay, not happening. I am so not becoming another notch."

"Shelby, I like you, you know I do."

"I bet you 'like' a lot of girls Clay. I like you too... as a friend." Shelby leaned forward off of Clays chest. "I'm sorry if I'm giving you the wrong impression. Can we head back now? Danny has had to finish playing by now."

Clay reluctantly moved back to his original driving position and drove them back.

Liz and Ricky were already back and eating off of paper plates. Sara and Danny were filling their own plates when Shelby and Clay joined than at the food table.

"How was football?" Sara asked.

"Your sister threw the winning touchdown." Clay told Sara proudly.

"Wow, really, you are such a jock!" Sara teased Shelby.

"How was hockey Danny?"

"It was great, we kept winning. My legs feel like rubber bands right now."

They joined Liz and Ricky to eat and fill each other in on their fun afternoon.

The dinner food was put away along with the grills. People changed out of their day clothes into attire more suitable to dancing in a chilly barn. The band struck up and played a little bit of everything. Country western songs that everyone lined danced to including Sara and Shelby who, under Liz's tutelage, had fun trying to stay with everyone else. Pop tunes and Mo town songs that dancers free-styled too. Sara and Shelby were both good dancers and Clay noticed that they both turned heads when they danced. The slow songs were killing Shelby. Clay had Shelby feeling warm and tingly as he fit their warm bodies together swaying sensuously.

"You aren't like other girls." Clay whispered softly into her ear.

Shelby snuggled in closer as her hips rocked across his jeans. Her entire body was firing hormonal warning signs. She was in serious trouble with this guy. He made her feel special. Her battle to keep her distance was slowly ebbing away.

Liz was dancing a slow song with Ricky. They weren't physically close like Shelby and Clay were; but they were talking and laughing with each other during the songs. Shelby motioned to Clay with a tap and she and Clay anxiously watched Lars as he approached the unsuspecting couple. Clay tensed, ready to help Ricky, but Shelby rubbed his shoulders and held him at bay.

Lars looked at Liz. "May I cut in?"

Liz looked at Ricky and said, "Do you mind?"

Ricky, being of sound mind and body, reluctantly handed Liz over to Lars. Ricky looked at Shelby and Clay, shrugged and went on to quickly find another dance partner.

"Well that didn't take him long." Shelby said.

"I told Ricky this might happen. He only likes Liz as a friend. He told me he'd never talked to her much before and she's a sweet girl."

"I hope Lars thinks so." Shelby said quietly.

The song ended and Shelby noticed Lars leading Liz away from their little group. The band played for a good two hours before taking a well deserved break, much to the disappointment of the partiers. Shelby was sitting on a bale of hay alone, while Sara and Danny shared one next to her. Clay had gone off to refill their beers. Shelby saw Lars and Liz holding hands as they walked towards her. They stopped right in front of Shelby; a small tremor of fear tickled her spine. She really didn't know what to expect.

Lars spoke first. His voice was hushed and he was clearly uncomfortable. "Um Shelby, I'm really sorry for hitting you."

"You hit my sister!" Sara jumped up ready for battle, but Danny pulled her back, recognizing the man was apologizing.

"I don't know what the hell I was think. I've never hit a woman. You just were squirming all over the place, I couldn't get to you, and I sort of kicked into game mode."

Clay arrived back just then and quietly gave everyone their cups and placed his to the side, he didn't sit, and his eyes remained on Lars.

Liz elbowed Lars in his ribs. "I'm sorry for what I said too. I know you won't believe this but I'm usually not like that."

Lars then looked at Clay. "I'm really sorry Clay I didn't mean to deck your girl. Really I don't want any trouble between us. I don't know how to make it up to you." He said looking back to Shelby. "If you want to take a swing at me you can."

Shelby giggled relieving the tension that had domed the group. "Lars I'm not going to hit you."

Lars looked at Clay. "You want to deck me?

I won't hit back."

Shelby quickly stood up between the two hulking men so that she was standing with her back to Clay pressed to his front. She wrapped Clays arms around her stomach so she could hold them against her.

"Clay doesn't want to hit you either, right Clay?" She answered for him quietly.

Clay was still reeling from Shelby's affectionate move that he was barely thinking. His anger towards Lars had dissipated because Shelby had simply held him.

His numb brain recovered so he answered. "Yea, no man, we're good. Liz you good?"

Shelby loved how he thought about her. Clay really was a good guy.

"I'm good." Liz smiled at both of them. "Shelby I had fun meeting you today. I hope we can get together again before you leave."

"I'd like that." Shelby said and meant it.

"Lars is taking me home now."

Lars grunted.

"My brother is waiting in the car."

"That aught to be a fun ride home." Shelby teased.

Lars shot Shelby a quirky smile.

"Yea, if you see me on the road just run me over because that means what I have to say to her brother did not go over well." Shelby laughed and Liz patted Lars on the chest.

The wonderful party was drawing to a close. Clay got the truck and they piled in tired from the days events. When they arrived back to Shelby's Mom's ranch Clay's dad was there. The four of them sat and talked to them for a bit and then Sara and Danny headed off to bed. Clay asked Shelby to walk him out. They stood by Clays truck facing each other

"Shelby, I had a great time today."

"I had fun too."

"I'd like to see you again?"

"Clay, we talked about this. I like being with you. I have fun with you. I'm not going to be a notch in your cowboy belt."

"Wow, you don't think very highly of me do you." Clay spat out more forcefully than he meant to.

Shelby put her hand on his arm and gave it a squeeze.

"Clay, it's because I do think so much of you." Shelby looked into his gorgeous green eyes and fingered a forlorn lock of his dark hair off his forehead.

"Yea, right."

"Listen please understand, I had a really good time today. It was a good time because I was with you. You made it fun. You made it special."

"So what's the problem, Shel's?"

"Clay, I saw how every girl looked at you. Don't think I didn't notice how they would touch you, brush against you. You can pick and choose from any chickie around. I'd like to hang out with you more while I'm here. I just know if we became more than friends..." Shelby looked right into Clays green eyes. "Clay, you would end up breaking my heart, and I've been there done that."

"Shelby, come on. I would never hurt you. Maybe you would break my heart. We had a great day. I didn't want to be with anyone but you. I tried to show you that today. I know sometimes the girls flirt, but I thought I did a good job keeping them at a distance?"

"Clay, that's just it. I don't want to cramp your style, so to speak."

"That's just crap Shelby."

"Crap or not, we are friends and I hope we can remain friends. I want to visit my Mom and not feel uncomfortable when the neighbors visit." Shelby nudged Clay with her elbow.

Clay looked down at Shelby. She was so much smaller than him. He had felt protective of her all night. Fact was that she could totally take care of herself though. She proved that when she kneed Lars one of the biggest guy in the county in his nuts. His friends had asked if she was with him, like as a girlfriend, and he had told them, yes she was with his. She'd probably kill him if she knew that, but there was no way he was giving his friends a green light when it came to her. He had told her as much. She made him laugh, she was smart, she was sweet, and she was great looking. He didn't think she had any idea how beautiful she was; blond hair, a fan fucking-tastic, curvaceous body, and her eyes, geez Caribbean ocean blue.

Clay noticed they reflected her every mood. When she was being competitive they sparked and darkened. When she was laughing they lightened and brightened. God, he wondered what they'd look like when she was coming. Clay adjusted his stance as his cock began to demand more room in his jeans.

Clay took off his cowboy hat and ran one hand through his black hair. "I want to see you while your here, so I'll try to be 'just a friend', but I'm telling you Shel's, chemistry is chemistry." Shelby cocked her head to the side. "That means darling, you can't always control what comes natural."

Clay dipped his head and pressed a warm, sweet kiss on Shelby's mouth that she had been totally unprepared for. Before she could protest, he had pulled back. He then swiped her stunned plush lips with his thumb, got in his truck and took off.

Shelby watched him leave. His kiss

had been brief but she had felt it clear to her toes. Shit, she thought, I'm in deep shit! She then laughed because she remembered his mischievous twinkle in his eyes as he ended the kiss. Okay round one to Clay.

Chapter 3

The next night Clay and his Dad took the Jensen girls and Danny to dinner. It was Sara and Danny's last night and Clays Dad wanted to send them off right. Grace had finally told her daughters that she'd been seeing his Dad and Clay was happy that he didn't have to keep that secret any longer. Shelby had pretty much figured it out and she was okay with it. Which to Clay, spoke volumes regarding how much she loved her mother. He knew it wasn't easy for Shelby to see her Mom with someone other than her dad, but Shelby didn't make her Mom feel bad or guilty, she just rolled with it. It made Clay like her even more.

In the truck Clay couldn't sit by Shelby because they had to sit three to a bench but he kept looking back at her. She'd meet his eyes and a little blush would christen her cheeks before she looked away. At the restaurant he made sure he was sitting right next to her. He kept his leg firmly against hers the entire dinner. They talked about what was on the menu, football, the party, and life in general. Clay and Shelby didn't even hear the waitress tell the table what the specials were. They were both so wrapped up in each other.

Sara and Danny were leaving the next day and Clay offered to drive them to the airport for Grace. He wanted to show Shelby around State and Shelby had agreed to go with him. Grace said that was fine. She wasn't a fan of airport goodbyes. Clays Dad told him that bad weather was coming in and to be smart about driving. Clay and Shelby talked about their adventure to State the rest of the meal. They decided to spend the night there since it was a long drive.

The next morning Clay picked Shelby,

Sara, and Danny up at Graces. Grace said a tearful goodbye to Sara and Danny and then Grace hugged Shelby and told her to be careful and smart. Clay thought it might have had a double meaning like, 'don't get too close to Clay', but he couldn't be sure. Clay really liked Grace and knew she just wanted their families to get on well together. He couldn't blame her. He did have a reputation with the ladies and Grace had seen him in action. Grace then hugged Clay and told him to be careful. Clay knew then he was correct. Grace's eyes implored him to be careful with her little girl.

Their day had started off so well. They had gotten Sara and Danny to the airport on time, then they checked into a local hotel. Shelby raised an eyebrow when she saw they were sharing a room. Clay had smiled and said, "Hey, one can only hope." She laughed at his persistence.

Shelby continued to keep her distance from Clay physically although it was like keeping a magnet from steel. They had walked around campus arm in arm, but when he tried to hold her hand she gave him that, 'no we already went ' look. They toured the campus and Shelby saw Clays and Jed's team pictures hanging in the Athletic Center. They ate a late breakfast in a quaint luncheonette that was crammed with photos of States football team dating back through the decades. Shelby found Clay to be intelligent and witty. He was kind, good natured, loyal, and 'Good God' he was handsome. Begrudgingly, Shelby admitted to herself, that she was having mixed feelings about Clay. What if he was the one? Her warring Shelby's, sensible and carefree were almost singing the same tune.

On one hand, carefree Shelby wanted to take a chance and have a romantic fling with the gorgeous man. On the other hand the sensible Shelby, told her to hang in there for a little longer and not give in to her lustful thoughts. She was leaving in less than a week. Who knows when she'd even see him again? Nope, she needed sensible Shelby to win the mind bending schizophrenic battle raging with in her. She needed to keep her distance from Clay. He'd break her heart.

The snow had started falling and they had ensconced themselves in a local bar with a group of Clays friends. State was on break so the clientele was older. The jukebox was kicking out lively tunes, and Shelby stood by the bar with a beer, enjoying the music, listening to Clay and his friends. Shelby fit right in with his friends. He knew his friends liked her too. One guy asked if they were a couple. This time Shelby heard Clay's response. Clay had playfully put his arm around her and drew her close telling his friend she was all his. They ribbed him commenting that, 'he always got all the good ones.' Shelby cringed at the reference to him having many other women.

Clay had kept his arm around her. Shelby leaned comfortably into his welcoming chest. He leaned down to nuzzle her neck, just under her ear. "You smell wonderful." He murmured huskily against her skin. Shelby's inner turmoil splintered, sensible Shelby was nudged to the curb. Maybe it was the alcohol; maybe it was because he was so persistent. Shelby's nipples pebbled under his penetrating gaze and she turned her traitorous body to lean into his. He was so much taller than her. She only came up to his chest.

Shelby looked up at Clay her hooded eyes conveying all Clay needed to know right then. He tilted her chin up and swept into her mouth. His tongue licked her closed lips until she granted him the access they both craved. They moaned simultaneously into each other's mouth. Clay tightened his hold on her possessively. The kiss conveyed so much emotion that Shelby felt herself melt into his arms. She pushed her hips towards him without even realizing she was doing it.

Clay's cock was granite hard. He turned his body in towards the bar bringing her with him. She felt his steel rod press firmly where she needed it most. The wanton move shook Shelby back to reality. She placed her hands on his chest and pushed him slightly away. Not so much that their lower halves weren't still papered hip to knee. Shelby felt his hard length press against her stomach.

"Clay." She managed to eek out a little breathlessly. "PDA to much PDA." Clay planted a light kiss on her lips. He grabbed her ass, picking her up to gently plop her on a barstool. Still unable to face anyone with his raging hard on, Clay remained standing between her thighs. Shelby let him. He tucked a strand of blond hair carefully behind Shelby's ear as he leaned in to her putting his cheek next to hers. "You are not like other girls." He repeated what he had said when they had been dancing.

The rest of the night Clay remained close to Shelby always touching her in some way. Shelby was mentally kicking her own ass for letting him kiss her. Problem was she had thoroughly enjoyed it. She searched for sensible Shelby to reappear but to no avail. She was thoroughly smitten with her cowboy-rancher. They were acting like a couple and Shelby liked that too, too much. She allowed the fairy tale to continue.

The festive group moved to a table and ordered food. They continued to drink and dance. Shelby loved being with Clay. She loved feeling like his girl. He made her feel special with the attention he heaped on her. Always touching her, and often sliding his lips to her neck, face, even hands. He was a very sensual man and he was rocking Shelby to her core. Carefree Shelby had won the war and was lustfully thinking about the hotel room waiting for them later that night. She was an adult. He was an adult. Why not enjoy him while she was here. Just touching him sent shivers through her.

Clay left the table to order more

drinks. Shelby watched him. He was achingly handsome, out of her league even. Was she acting irrationally, pretending they were a couple? He had a spectacular backside all firm and tight, she could see herself holding him to her as he slid into her. His shoulders were wide and tapered down to a trim waist. She had never seen him with his shirt off, yet she knew he would be spectacular, packed with lean muscles that didn't come from a gym but from active work. He moved with grace, yet he was so masculine. He owned his area. Wherever he walked, he turned heads. Girls gave him flirtatious glances as he neared, and guys that he didn't know respected his space and gave him berth.

While Clay was at the bar a beautiful, long legged, well - endowed girl stepped up to him. Shelby watched with interest, he'd been wonderful all day, when women made passes at him. He always politely nodded towards her with a smile and said he was with his girl. It made Shelby gooey. This girl, however, must have been different. First thing Shelby noticed was how she touched him, intimately. Her hands cupped his backside then grasped his hips as she pressed up suggestively against his back with her front. One of the girls at the table commented. "There's Candy." Nodding in Clay and the girl's direction. "Who?" Asked Shelby. The girl answered, "One of Clays girlfriends." A nauseating bolt shook through Shelby. She watched Clay turn around holding the drinks in both hands. The bombshell flung her arms around his neck and kissed him passionately on the lips, her body rubbing against him provocatively. Clay was balancing the drinks as the kiss continued for what seemed like an eternity to Shelby. She looked away embarrassed. God she was a freak-in moron. Excusing herself from the table, she grabbed her coat from the rack by the entrance door and ran outside. She didn't know what to do or even where to go. She just knew she needed distance. The cold snow continued to fall, the wind whipping at her unbuttoned coat. She put her head down to forge through the wind and headed down the block hoping to get her bearings. Shelby needed to get back to the hotel. She chastised herself vehemently for allowing herself to 'play' couple with Clay. Then she got angry with Clay. WTF she thought. He'd been attentive, kissing, touching her all day and the first girlfriend he sees he kisses and while she was sitting right there. He was an arrogant ass!

Back at the bar Clay had disentangled himself from Candy's lip locking embrace. He hadn't been able to remove himself from her clutches as quickly as he would have liked because he had the drinks in his hands and he was wedged between two bar stools so he hadn't even been able to turn away from her.

"Candy, what are doing?" He still held the two beers but half their contents had spilt over the rim onto his hands.

"Clay honey, aren't you glad to see me?"

"Candy, we talked. I like you as a friend, we had good times, but I'm here with someone else. Someone I really care about."

"Who, I don't see anyone near you." Candy continued to rub up against him.

"She's over..." Clay didn't see Shelby at the table anymore.

"Shit!"

Clay pushed Candy aside with his forearms not caring that even more beer sloshed over the sides and went to the table.

"Guys where's Shelby?"

"Uh, bathroom?" one girl said.

"No, she headed for the door." One of his friends countered.

"Why didn't you stop her?"

"Dude you were lip locked with

Candy, we thought, you know, you were trying to send Shelby a message."

"Shit!" Clay repeated. He put the almost empty glasses on the table and grabbed his coat and ran out the door.

Shelby needed a cab. She was pissed. Crap in Jersey she'd find a cab. Here in friggin Wyoming she'd have more luck hailing a horse. Realizing how ridiculous it was to be walking around in the crazy ass snowstorm, Shelby ducked into the first bar boasting a welcome sign. It was a bit of a dive, but it was warm. The only one in the entire place was a bartender. Perfect, she didn't want company. She went to the bar and hoisted herself onto the stool and ordered a beer as she tried to regroup.

She had known he was a player. She should have kept Clay at friend status. Shelby had simply let her libido take over. She felt like an idiot. She just could not understand how he could go from sweet and attentive to making out with another girl in a matter of minutes. His friends must be having quite a laugh at her expense right now. No one had tried to even stop her when she left. She sickened again at the image of Clay kissing the leggy girl.

Shelby was nursing her beer and fiddling with her cocktail napkin. She failed to notice the two leather clad bikers that had strolled in. They closed in on either side of her, which jolted her back from her self-reprimanding. They reeked of alcohol, reefer, and motor oil.

"Hey Missy you need a refill?" The smaller biker asked as he pressed his chest against her back. Shelby looked from one man to the other. Geez could this night get worse. These jerks were seriously pulling this shit. Shelby was small but she took no crap, no matter who was dishing it.

"You miss the health class about self

space?" She glared at the rude biker as she tried to stand up to leave.

"Ha-ha! I like that. You're feisty." The other biker chimed in.

Shelby looked down the bar towards the bartender to see he had disappeared. She was on her own with these morons.

"Boys you need to go find someone else to play with. I've had a shit day."

Shelby was on her feet and heading for the door.

The larger of the men grabbed Shelby by the arm and pulled her back so she crashed roughly against his barrel like chest. "We kind'a like playing with you."

"Let go of me you ass hole." Shelby kicked him in the shins but it didn't seem to affect him. Crap, not good she thought. A prickle of real fear had her feeling the hair rise on the back of her neck. The other A-hole was enjoying the show, laughing, calling out instructions like, "Try to kiss her" and "does she got big tits?"

Shelby tried to wrench her arm free but the bulky man had a firm grip on her. She looked for the bartender hoping he had returned. Panic gripped Shelby, she was really in trouble here. A loud thud had her and her drunken detainer turning to see what had made the noise. The smaller, mouthy biker was knocked out cold under a nearby table, and very lethal looking Clay was shaking out a hand, a hand that had obviously put the smaller biker where he lay.

Clay closed his large hand over the large bikers thick, leather - encased forearm, ripping his hand off of Shelby's arm. Shelby moved away quickly to stay out of his reach and stumbled awkwardly to the floor landing hard on her butt. Clay and the biker were trading serious blows. Shelby watched Clay land punches that had the biker grunting as they landed. The biker picked up a chair and Clay turned to deflect the blow with a raised arm his shoulder taking the brunt of the blow as the chair shattered on impact. Clay launched himself at the biker gripping the biker's leather coat and heaving him against the bar. The inebriated bikers head snapped back from the force of his body hitting the bar. Clay took advantage by landing a brutal punch to the large man's solar plexus. He then finished the staggering man off with a devastating blow to his chin; an upper cut that cracked the biker's head back. Shelby heard bones crack and knew Clay had just busted the ass holes jaw. The large bikers eyes rolled to the back of his head and he slumped to the floor unconscious.

Shelby remained on the floor. Clay flexed his shoulder that had been hit with the chair and shook his hand out again. Clays knuckles were scraped and he a welt emerging under his eye. He stepped back from the bar, breathing hard. Shelby could see that Clay's posture was rigid. Waves of adrenalin coursed off him. His eyes were wild and sizzled with anger. Clay stepped to

Shelby and helped her up. He released her hand once she was standing.

Clays jaw was set tight as he inspected her from head to toe. Shelby began to shiver uncontrollably. Clay had found her, beat the shit out of two men, one of them significantly larger, and he saved her sorry ass. Shelby also realized if he hadn't she would have been in serious trouble. Clay ran his hand through his hair, and then abruptly turned from her. Seeing him turn from her crushed Shelby. She dropped her head into her hands and softly began to cry into her hands. Clay heard her and his heart crumbled.

When Clay couldn't find her he was beyond worried. He was pissed Candy had kissed him. He'd been honest with her when he broke it off with her last month. Candy had been fun but he didn't want a relationship with her and he knew she did. He figured she'd seen Shelby with him and had been trying to start trouble. Clay had been looking into every doorway searching for Shelby.

When he opened the door to the bar and saw the bikers and then Shelby, his gut clenched. When he saw one of them had his hands on her he lost it.

Clay rubbed his hands over his face. He needed to control his emotions. He didn't want to scare Shelby. His first instinct had been to hug her, then throw her over his shoulder like a cave man claiming his woman. Clay knew that wouldn't go over so well, so he reigned in his testosterone.

He turned back to Shelby and extended a hand to her. She took it, wiped her tears with her free hand and they left the bar together. He walked her back to his car and drove them to the hotel without uttering one word. Shelby didn't feel like saying anything either. She had too many emotions coursing through her. God help her she was jealous and hurt that Clay kissed the other girl. She had been frightened when the biker had grabbed her. She was relieved when Clay found her. She was scared for him when he was fighting. She was upset with herself for making Clay get in the fight. The worse feeling was that she was terrified that Clay now hated her.

Back in the room Shelby shucked off her coat and boots and faced Clay with a hand on her hip. Her stature was an attempt to appear unfazed even though she was crumbling inside.

"Clay, thank you. I'm sorry you had to fight. I didn't ... I didn't think. I'm really sorry." Shelby's voice shook under duress and her chin began to quiver as she tried not to cry. She sniffled and continued speaking.

"You don't need to stay here with me. You can go back to your friends. I'm just going to watch TV. I don't want to wreck your night."

It took Clay two steps before he could pull her tight against him. His arms wrapped around her cradling her to him. He drew her head against his chest and rested his chin on the top of her head.

"Jesus, Shelby, do you know how scared I was when I couldn't find you."

Shelby dissolved into tears. She was shocked. This was not what she expected him to say. Her body shook with heavy sobs.

"You saved me." She sobbed out, still pressed to his chest.

"Why would you leave? We were having fun. I thought we were having fun." Clays voice was fraught with anxiety.

Shelby gulped her tears back.

"Clay, you were kissing a girl. I didn't want to, you know, like I told you before, 'cramp your style'."

Clay continued to hold her to him. He sighed knowing she had seen the kiss. He knew how it must have looked to her.

Candy's timing was shit.

"If you had stuck around you would have heard me tell her I was with someone. Someone I care about." Clay said softly as he caressed her cheek.

"Clay it crushed me to see you kissing her. I know we aren't really a couple, but we'd been playing at it all afternoon. I guess I was so caught up in how nice it felt, that I forgot it wasn't real."

"Shel's, I wasn't playing." Clay sighed and Shelby felt some tension drain from him.

"Clay don't. Please, I can't do this. I told you it was a bad idea."

"You have to Shelby, I'm not letting go. What the hell were you doing in that bar?"

"I was cold. I needed to think."

"What if I had gone the other way looking for you? Shit, those are not good guys. They could have..." Clays voice betrayed his emotion.

Shelby put her chin on Clays chest to peer up at him. Her arms were around his back. He was so handsome it literally took her breath away.

"Thank you for coming to find me, Clay. Are you hurt?"

"No baby. I'm okay. I was just scared when I saw you with those guys. Shelby that girl you saw back at the bar. She's an old girlfriend. She's nothing to me. I need you to know that."

Clay looked down at Shelby and her heart skipped a beat. He stroked her lips then leaned down for a kiss. This wasn't like the kiss in the bar, this one rocked Shelby, and she melted into him. Clay was demanding. His mouth captured hers and his tongue stroked and worked hers until she moaned with raw desire.

Clay picked Shelby up under her ass. She wrapped her legs around his waists and he walked them to the bed. They continued to explore each other with their hands as their tongues fought for dominance. Clay was so hard he felt his jeans zipper imprinting on his cock. He placed his hand under Shelby's chin and forced her to look at him.

His voice was ragged as he fought for control. "Shel's, I want to be with you more than you can even imagine, but I want you to want it too."

Shelby knew Clay deserved her honesty. She wanted him to understand how she felt.

"I'm afraid Clay. I don't want to get hurt. I'm not a one and done girl. I don't know what this is. What we are." Shelby paused and dragged in a breath. "I do know you make me want more, more time, more kisses, more you."

Clay bookended her face with his

hands and dropped her forehead to hers. "I want more too, Shel's. We can do this. We can have more." He whispered huskily.

Shelby slid her hands into Clays hair and pulled him down so she could kiss him. Right before she devoured him she murmured, "More."

Chapter 4

Clay slid his hands up the side of Shelby's face until his hands were entwined in her soft hair. He continued to make love to her mouth with his tongue. Shelby was making little moaning sounds that were driving him crazy. He needed to touch her, everywhere. He broke from her lips for only long enough to reached behind his neck and pulled his shirt off. Shelby's hands went directly to his back. She caressed his skin running her fingers along his contoured muscles. She played with his sculpted muscles running her fingers around the bulging grooves. Clay pushed his hands under her top and pushed up. Shelby got the message that he wanted her shirt off too. She pushed at Clay indicating she wanted to sit up. He moved to accommodate her and watched as she took off her shirt. Neither took their eyes off each other. The pent up energy between them crackled. Clay stood up next to the bed and helped her up. There was no need for words. They were panting from their explosive kiss and they both knew where this was headed.

Clay slipped his fingers under her bra straps and pulled them down slowly. His fingers scraped along the sides of her heavy breast, when the straps where near her bicep Clay traced the front edge of the lacy material. Shelby's nipples were so distended they ached. Clay sucked them through the thin material and Shelby moaned her approval. Clay reached behind her and unfastened the binding contraption. When it loosened completely, Clay pulled it away from her body. Shelby felt her breasts prickle in anticipation. Clay put his hand under one breast and bent his head to kiss her with an open mouth right on her nipple. Shelby almost came right there. She was warm all over. Her body was achy and tingling. Her lower half was a complete dichotomy. How could she be so wet yet feel like she was on fire.

Clay maintained eye contact and unsnapped his belt and his jeans. He sat on the bed and took off his cowboy boots and his socks. His cock was huge, wonderfully rimmed with a bulbous head, thick and veined and standing eagerly against his abdomen. He reached to Shelby's waist and unsnapped her jeans and pulled them below her knees. Her little white lacy thong underwear remained in place. He patted the bed encouraging her to sit next to him. When she did he took off her boots and socks and then completely pulled her pants off. Except for the lacy triangle over her mound, she was naked. Clay scooted back on the bed and pulled Shelby with him.

They were lying facing each other. Clay was mesmerized with her perfect little body. It was soft, yet toned. She had curves and a flat stomach that slightly sloped to the area below he couldn't wait to taste. Clay traced his hands down her side and back up again. He lightly stroked her breasts, and then slowly circled her dusky areola, before finally tracing his calloused fingertips over her nipple. Shelby moaned under his ministrations. Shelby was doing the same with Clays magnificent body. She traced over the ridges and muscles with her fingers sweetly exploring his hard body. She reached up to his jaw, his cheeks, and then seductively traced his lips with her finger. Clay sucked the fingers into his mouth and lightly teased them with his tongue. The sensation was so heady Shelby had to close her eyes. Clay reached down and swept his fingers over the top of her thong between her legs. He felt the heated moisture and his cock pulsed in anticipation as he quickly tugged them off her.

Clay leaned up on his forearm that was underneath him and reached to the other side of Shelby with his other arm so he was on top of her. Shelby opened her legs to make room for him. Clay leaned on his forearms so his weight wouldn't totally rest on her. He framed her face again with his hands and looked into her ocean blue eyes.

"Are you sure?" He asked in a husky whisper.

Shelby was quaking with arousal. Her nipples were pointy and begging to be touched. Her folds were slick and she could feel her own juices on her inner thigh. She reached up and pulled Clay down for a sensual, slow, tongue tangled kiss. She pulled back, noticing how Clays eyes were holding hers. He was making sure she was okay. The powerful realization had Shelby mist up and Clay swiped his thumb to wipe away the errant tear.

"Its okay baby, we don't have to do anything. I love holding you. It's enough."

"Clay, I want to. I'm not use to someone being so thoughtful."

Clay dropped his forehead to hers and

then pressed a sweet tender kiss to her mouth. When he released her lips Shelby whispered.

"Clay, make love to me, please make love to me."

Clay looked at Shelby with nothing short of adoration on his face. He smiled down at her and leaned in for another kiss. It was so full of passion Shelby almost couldn't breathe. Clay kissed his way down her torso stopping along the way to lick and suckle her breasts, tits, hips and belly button. He reached her mound and pushed his hands under her ass lifting her up, exposing her most intimate place to him fully. Clay sucked in a breath seeing her pink folds. Her small rose - colored clit nestled like a treasure inside her delicate lips that were shiny with moisture.

"God, you're fucking perfect." He whispered.

He shimmied to the bottom of the bed

and stood up reaching for her hips. Shelby didn't know what he wanted so she let him show her. Clay gently dragged her towards the end of the bed. Her ass was still on the mattress, but just barely. He took her feet and planted them wide, holding her ankles. Shelby looked at his face with a quizzical expression.

"I'm too tall and I want to spend some time down here. Just getting comfortable." Clay knelt down on the carpet leaving him face level with her sheening pussy.

Shelby sucked in a breath when what he had said sunk in, but by that time Clay had stuck his head between her legs and was exploring her feverishly with his tongue. Shelby was squirming and little sexy moans were escaping her slightly parted lips. Clay licked her creamy slit from top to bottom and then back down again. He circled her hard pink nub with his rough tongue, but didn't touch it. Shelby was delirious with need. Clay flat tongue lapped his way down to her core where he drove it furiously inside of her. Shelby was tightening like a bow. Clay took his hands off her ankles and opened her lips with his middle fingers. He then took his thumb's placing them on both side of her clit pressing on it gently using an up down motion. Shelby was headed towards an orgasm of incredible depth. Her face and chest were flush with color and she could feel the tiny spasm start along her vaginal wall.

"Clay, please Clay, Oh my God Clay." Shelby sat up abruptly. Clay sat back on his heels, releasing her clit in surprise. Shelby wiggled quickly off the end of the bed molding her legs around his torso. She slide down his body, holding his strong shoulders while her distended clit rubbed every taunt muscle on his chiseled stomach. She took one hand off his shoulder reaching between them, grabbing Clays cock. He gasped with her touch. Shelby guided his engorged cock into her small core. Slowly she pushed down, inch by inch, on his granite hard throbbing length until she had taken him fully. His size stretched her and her clit rubbed erotically in the hair above his staff. Shelby sucked in a ragged breath. Clay gripped her hips and licked the seam of her slightly opened mouth with his tongue until she let him in to play. The sensation was over whelming, Clay hadn't even pumped into her. Shelby exploded, her body arched back against the bed thrusting her nipples out to press against Clays chest. She whimpered his name as her slick inner walls sucked greedily on his cock. Clay started pumping upwards into her rippling core. He felt her insides gripping his shaft, his balls, wet with her juices tightened. She was so hot, so liquid, and perfectly molded around his cock. Clay tried to hold off so he could give Shelby more, but he couldn't. Her rapture had triggered his. He burst inside of her choking out her name. He continued to pump into her releasing every drop.

Clay held his forehead to Shelby's. "Holy shit, Shelby." He pressed a kiss to her

lips then her nose then back to her lips.
"Woman, that was hot." Shelby still couldn't
talk. Clay pulled back from her face to make
sure she was okay. They both were panting
and coated with a shiny layer of sweat.
"Shel's?"

"I'm okay. That was... Like you
said...hot."

"Why did you stop me? I wanted to
make you come with my tongue."

Shelby felt a tingle inside her. This
man ignited a fire in her that wouldn't stop
raging. "I wanted our first time to be
together."

Clay looked down at her and then fell
backwards onto the carpet bringing her with
him so she was on top of him. They remained
connected. He was smiling from ear to ear.
Shelby traced his smile with her fingertips.

"What are you smiling about?"

"I like that you said first time. That

you know it's not our last."

Shelby looked over at him shy like. "I didn't mean to sound presumptuous. I know I'm only here for a week."

"Oh darling, I want to make love to you so many more times, in so many different ways in this next week." Clay gently brought Shelby's face to his to bestow a deep and intoxicating kiss on her plump pink lips. Her released her and swept his thumbs over her cheeks as he devoured her eyes with his.

"I don't want you to forget me when you go back to New Jersey." Clay said with a sad sigh.

Shelby pushed her fingers through his now sex tousled hair, her thumbs lying gently at his temples. "I don't think that's going to be the problem big guy." Shelby said a little sadly.

Chapter 5

They remained in bed and ordered room service when they got hungry. They made love again. Clay got his wish and made Shelby come with his tongue. Shelby returned the favor but before she could make him come he twirled her little body up and over his so he could suck on her clit while she continued to hoover on him, less than a minute later they combusted together. Shelby swallowed Clay's salty semen as her hips convulsed and Clays pumped. Clay nipped her clit with his teeth while he was coming forcing her to come a second time.

When they weren't pleasuring each other they held each other and talked. Neither wanted the night to end. Before it got too late Clay decided to call home to check in with his dad. When he couldn't reach him he called his Aunt Betty who had helped raise him when his Mom had just up and left him and his dad. Clay had been just a baby. He still talked to her but he didn't really think of her as his Mom. Betty had more than made up for the lack of biological maternal love and Clay loved her like she was his real mom. Betty answered the phone and Clay knew just from the tone in her voice something was wrong.

"Hey Aunt Betty, I've been trying to reach dad. Everything okay?" Clay listened quietly. Shelby sensed something was seriously wrong so she sat up draped only in the top sheet and rested her head on Clay's wide shoulder. She could only hear one side of the conversation.

"Is she okay?"

"Yea, I got it."

"This sucks."

"I'll tell her."

"If you talk to Dad, tell him I love him

and I'll be careful."

"Love you too Aunt Betty, thanks. Will do." Clay hung the phone up and turned to Shelby who was pensively sitting next to him. Her eyes were wide open. She knew bad news was coming.

"Shel's I don't want you to panic and before I say anything more your Mom is going to be okay."

"Oh God, Mom. What happened?"

"There was a fire in her barn. I don't know much more than that but she's okay and she's at the hospital. My dad is with her."

"Can we go?"

"No baby, I'm sorry the storm is still bad. My Dad says to wait until morning. He promises she's okay."

"Did Betty say if she was burned? Are her animals okay?"

"I don't know. Trust me baby if she were bad I'd get you there. My Dad has a pretty level head, well except when it comes to your Mom. You have to know he's head over heels for her. I've never seen him like this. It's like she's his air."

Shelby cupped Clay's cheek then laid her head on her chest as he pulled her to him. "I trust him Clay. We'll wait until morning. I'm just worried, she's all Sara and I have."

When morning came Clay and Shelby assessed the roads and decided to head to the hospital. It was in Briggsby so they had a good two - hour drive. It had stopped snowing and even though many roads were still snow covered they decided it was safe enough to leave. Shelby was worried about her Mom, as was Clay. When they arrived at the hospital they found Clays Dad holding Shelby's Mom, both were sound asleep. Shelby quickly assessed how her Mom looked and relief flooded her when she realized her injuries were not life altering. Clay had been looking Grace over as well and Shelby saw him breath a sigh of relief. They didn't want to wake them so they quietly got on the empty bed next to Grace's and without realizing it succumbed to sleep lying in the same positions as their parents were in.

A few hours later Shelby heard her Mom and Jed talking. Shelby yawned, "Just wanted to let you know you had company." As she had thought Jed and her Mom didn't even realize she and Clay were there and she was correct as both parents' heads snapped towards her voice.

Shelby left Clays comfortable arms to walk to her Mom's bed. Jed got off the bed carefully so he wouldn't jostle Grace too much. He walked to Clay who now stood stretching out his long limbs. Jed gave Clay a hug and whispered. "You guys okay?"

"Yea, she was upset." Clay told his Dad, "But she's an emotional rock."

"Like her mother." Jed murmured, as he looked over to his 'everything' talking with her daughter.

"She's okay right?" Clay asked.

"Yea, bad head bump that required stitches, some burns, cuts, bruises. I want them to stay with us for a while."

"Sure, everything okay?"

"Someone set this fire Clay."

"Jesus, who? Why?"

"Don't know yet."

"The animals?"

"All accounted for and fine except cat. Can't find her. I didn't tell Grace."

"Okay. That would suck."

"Yea."

Grace and Shelby were engrossed in their own conversation. Jed politely interrupted and told them he and Clay were going to get coffee and they would be right back. Jed went to Grace and kissed her gently on her lips. He then looked at Shelby and gave her a little fatherly pat on her shoulder, which made Grace smile.

In the cafeteria Jed asked Clay about Shelby.

"Dad I really like her. Not sure how to explain it. She's fun to be with. It's not work. We like the same things. She's different."

Jed chuckled. "I get it Clay really I do. I'm just concerned because she is heading home in a few days. Grace told me she's concerned too. Shelby's been hurt before. She's not a casual fling kind of girl."

Clay laughed. "I know Shelby and I, we've had this conversation."

"Clay, this might not be the right time

but you have to know, I love Grace."

"I know Dad."

"I mean love her like I want to marry her."

"I think that's great Dad. You deserve to be happy. I know Mom wasn't a good wife. Shit, she wasn't even a good mother. Does Grace know how you feel?"

"I've told her that I love her. She doesn't know I want to marry her. Little worried about springing that on her." He chuckled.

"Don't worry Dad she loves you."

"That's why I'm concerned.

I want us to be a family, her family, my family, our family. If you and Shelby… You know if it ends badly."

"No pressure, huh Dad?" Clay teased, but them got serious. "I get it. But if you're asking me to back off, I can't. I know she's leaving soon. We're going to take things as they come."

Jed nodded. He'd raised a good man. They were both adults.

"Dad, she makes my insides twist up."

Jed laughed, a booming loud laugh that turned heads in the cafeteria.

"Oh son, you got it bad."

Jed and Clay returned with coffee for everyone. The nurse had checked Graces vitals and removed the catheter and IV. She told Grace the doctor would be in shortly and if he said she was okay, she could go home. They finished their coffees and Shelby and Clay entertained Jed and Grace with fun stories of their visit to State. Grace asked about the welt under Clays eye. Shelby looked to the floor awkwardly and nodded to Clay giving him silent permission to tell the story. Clay told them how an old girlfriend had grabbed him while he had been getting drinks at the bar.

"Cheerleader Candy?" Grace asked.

"You know her!" Shelby blurted out.

Grace laughed. "I saw her once, sweetie."

Shelby looked embarrassed and Clay dropped a hand on her thigh and gave her a quick squeeze. Clay continued with the story of Shelby leaving the bar and him tracking her down. Shelby jumped into the recounting to praise Clays heroics. He was playing it down. She told them that she thought she might have lost her license in the bar, since she couldn't find it anywhere. When they had finished the story Jed and Grace sat opened mouth gaping at them.

"Son, you could have been hurt. They could have had knives or guns. You know motor cycles clubs out don't recognize standard laws."

Shelby gasped thinking of what Clay had really risked saving her.

"Shelby what the hell were you thinking leaving that bar?"

"Mom!" Shelby exclaimed, clearly not happy with the reprimand.

"I wasn't thinking. I just... I just wasn't thinking. I was upset."

"I seem to remember another certain lady running from a bar." Jed said gently looking at Grace.

Grace sighed. "Sorry baby." Grace said to Shelby. "It's scary that's all." Grace looked at Clay.

"Clay thank - you."

Clay looked embarrassed. And luckily the conversation ended as the doctor came in and tried to shoo everyone from the room. Jed wasn't leaving Grace's side and was adamant about it. The doctor told Grace he needed to examine her thoroughly, hoping Grace could get Jed to leave. Jed told him he definitely wasn't leaving now. The doctor looked to Grace for guidance so Grace told Jed he could stay if he behaved and remained quiet. Jed grinned like he just won the lottery.

Shelby and Clay walked down to the lounge hand in hand. Shelby's head was down and it wasn't until Clay heard a soft sob that he realized she was crying.

"Babe, your Mom going to be alright."

"It's not that Clay. It's the fight. You could have been hurt. I could have gotten you hurt. I'm so sorry. If you'd gotten seriously hurt..." Shelby broke apart crying into her palms.

Clay took her hands and pulled them behind him so he could hold her. He rubbed his hands over her back trying to comfort her.

"Shelby, shhhh, babe, it's alright,

nothing happened. Stop crying, please your killing me." Shelby sniffed into his shirt. They were standing like that when Clays dad came to find them. Jed could tell she'd been crying. They looked up. Shelby wiped her eyes and asked about her Mom.

"She can leave. Will you help her get ready?"

When they were alone. Jed tilted his head in a questioning gesture.

"You need to tell me something, son?"

"It's okay Dad, she's upset that I could have been hurt by the bikers. You kind of knocked her for a loop talking about guns and knives."

"Oh, sorry, shit, but son, you could have been really hurt."

"Dad, I saw them touching her and I lost it. You would have done the same. They're lucky I left them breathing." Clay growled.

Jed clasped Clay's shoulders. "You always need to stay in control when women are involved. I know, trust me, I know it's hard. They have to be our first responsibility, especially now with some ass wipe gunning for our Grace. I need you Clay. We need to keep them safe while we figure out what the hell is going on, okay?"

Clay recognized his Dad was seriously worried about Grace. "Okay dad. We'll keep them safe."

Clay pulled his truck around to the front entrance and Jed helped Grace into the back and he got in the back with her. Shelby slide into the front seat and Clay reached for her hand and gave it a reassuring squeeze before starting to drive. Grace had told Shelby that they needed to stay at Jed and Clays for a while. Clay was going to drive them first to Graces house to collect some items and then they were headed back to 5 Star.

Chapter 6

The ride back was thankfully uneventful. Clay helped Shelby pack up some of her things and put them in his truck bed. While Shelby's Mom was walking to the truck she heard a meow and sure enough his dad found cat and she had had her kittens under Grace's front deck. Shelby and Clay ran back inside to get a box and a soft blanket for them. Clay tried to put the box with cat and her kittens in his truck bed for the short ride to his ranch but Grace firmly put her foot down and Clay's Dad ended up holding the box on his lap for the duration of the ride.

Back on the Five Star the only tense moment came when Clay's dad announced to him and Shelby that Grace was sleeping in his room and Clay and Shelby needed to deal with it as adults. Shelby, true to form made a funny comment about keeping the noise down, which relieved the tension in the air. Grace had looked positively green.

Clay put Shelby's clothes in the guest bedroom across the hall from his. Shelby walked in and wrapped her arms around him from behind.

"Thank you for bringing my things up for me. You know I could have stayed at my Mom's. I feel a little awkward imposing on you and your dad."

Clay stood up but didn't turn around. He loved the feeling of her pressed against his back with her cheek resting under his shoulder blade.

"You're welcome for bringing your things up and no, you could not have stayed at your Mom's. Shel's, who ever torched your Mom's barn and poisoned her sheep, mean business. My Dad is barely holding it together knowing she's in danger. There's no way your Mom would let you stay there anyway. Think of it as you're doing us a favor by keeping your Mom calm, which means my dads calm. Okay?"

"Yea, you're right. It's just, you know..."

Clay turned in her arms to face her.

"Don't say it Shelby."

"Say what?"

"You're going to tell me if I want to go out with my friends, I can. That I don't need to sit here with you."

"Crap, how did you know that? I'm pretty transparent aren't I?"

"I knew it because I'm beginning to understand you. You are headstrong and tough. You don't want to rely on anyone but yourself, yet everyone relies on you. You don't like drama in your life. You are a great friend and people like you instantly. You don't take any crap, which I assume gets you into trouble on occasion. You have had crappy boyfriends, so you have trust issues. You have no idea how gorgeous and desirable you are. You want to like me but you're afraid to let go. How'd I do?"

Shelby looked up at him, her mouth hung open in astonishment.

"Shit Clay why don't you just rip me open and dive in deeper." She said sheepishly.

"Babe, I plan to know everything about you. Remember... More, we can have more."

"How do you do that?"

"Do what?"

"Make me want to crawl into your lap and tell you my deepest darkest."

Clay laughed and pulled her down on his lap as he sat on the bed's edge.

"Okay you're in my lap, start talking."

Clay kissed her nose playfully. Shelby swatted his shoulder. "I want to know everything about you too, Clay."

"Well I can start by telling you that you are not sleeping in here, just your clothes are."

"Will that be okay? I mean..."

"Honey, our parents will probably not even know. They are far enough down the hall. I don't think we have anything to worry about."

"You don't think we'll hear them will we?"

"I don't know. My dad's never had a woman over."

Shelby looked at Clay. He knew she wanted to ask him something. Then he knew what it was she wanted to ask. He smiled brilliantly at her.

"And no babe, I've never had a girl in

my room either."

"Really?"

"Really."

Shelby relaxed in Clay's arms. Feeling content just holding him.

They were still pretty tired from the night before so they took a nap, in Shelby's new room. They had left the door open and their parents walked past and saw them lying together, sound asleep. Clay was on his back and Shelby was on her side with her head resting on Clays chest. Clays arm was possessively holding Shelby's hip. Jed signaled for Grace to be quiet and they slipped downstairs to let them continue sleeping.

The next couple days were filled with working on the ranch for Clay while Shelby attempted to pamper her mother. When they weren't working they spent every second together. They'd talk and take walks. Shelby helped with the animals and Clay loved seeing her working along side of him on his ranch. They spent every night making love and before the rooster crowed Shelby would jump out of Clays bed and dive into hers across the hall. Clay would get up to do chores and he would come into her room and kiss her senseless before going out to work.

New Years Eve was Monday night and Clay was taking Shelby to The Elks for the local bash. Their parents were staying in. Shelby surprised her Mom on Monday morning, informing her she was taking her in to Briggsby for a mani and pedi. The fire and prolonged exposure outside had done a number on her Mom's hands. Jed thought this was a good idea and offered to drive them. Shelby gave Clay a quick, 'help me' look.

"Hey dad why don't you let the girls have a little together time and you come help me with a couple of the bulls?"

Jed didn't look happy, but he finally agreed. The men put the girls in Clays truck and Jed reluctantly let Grace leave. Clay gave Shelby a light kiss on her lips and told her to be careful. Shelby loved the way Clay made her feel special.

The girls took off and Shelby told her Mom she wanted to do something for a girl she'd just met. Shelby explained to her Mom who Liz was and that she didn't have much female influence in her life. Shelby wanted to bring her to Briggsby and treat her to a mani - pedi. She didn't think Liz had ever had one. Shelby pulled into the post office and Grace went in to get directions to Liz's house.

Shelby parked in front of Liz's house and walked to the front door. She was greeted with barking and then the front door opened wide. A very large man stood in the open doorway.

"Hi, I'm Shelby Jensen, I'm a friend of

Liz's, is she home?"

The man didn't answer Shelby right away and she thought for sure this huge man was going to shoo her off his property. Instead he stepped away from the door beckoning Shelby inside as he bellowed up the staircase for Liz.

Shelby stepped inside and two dogs circled her legs. She knelt to them and scuffed them playfully behind their ears. Liz's dad watched her with intense eyes; she knew her actions were a test to her character that she needed to pass, for Liz's sake.

Liz bound down the stairs and bounced into Shelby's arms as she stood from petting the dogs.

"What are you doing here? I'm so glad to see you. Dad this is Shelby, the new friend I was telling you about."

Shelby stuck her hand out and Liz's dad accepted it and they shook. Shelby could see him slowly relaxing.

"It's very nice to meet you Mr. Dade. My Mom and I were wondering if we could borrow Liz for a few hours? We are going in to Briggsby and being new to the area we though Liz could guide us around." It was a little white lie but Shelby hoped it worked. She knew Liz's dad was quite strict.

"Oh Dad, can I go please?" Shelby found it a bit unnerving that a 24 year old needed to ask permission in this manner to go in to town, but she kept her mouth shut.

"You done with your chores?"

"Yes sir."

"You won't be too long?" Mr. Dade looked at Shelby.

"No sir my mother is with us. She's still recuperating from an accident. I won't be keeping her out long."

"Well, I guess it be okay. What are

you planning to do?"

Shelby didn't want to mislead Liz's dad and get Liz in trouble, so she was honest.

"Well first we are getting manicures and pedicures. Then I want to find an outfit to wear to the Elks tonight that's appropriate."

Mr. Dade's mouth hung open a bit.

"Oh!" squealed Liz. "I've never had one. That sounds great!"

Shelby watched Liz's dad's face soften as he witnessed her excitement.

"Do you have flip flop's? You'll need them for the pedicure."

"Yes, just give me two shakes and I'll be right back."

Liz ran back upstairs.

"No girl ever came here before to take Liz out. She said you were a nice girl. I thank you."

"Mr. Dade, really the pleasure is mine. There are not many girls who play a good game of football. At the party after Christmas we covered each other in the final game. That's how we become friendly."

"Yea, Liz told me. I'm even letting her go to the Elks party tonight. Larry, her brother and Lars are taking her. I guess she's growing up."

Liz bound down the steps at that exact time looking anything but grown up. Red faced with excitement, sweat pants and sweatshirt covering her lush curves, barn boots, and a long braid down her back completed her ensemble. Shelby had to suppress a giggle. Liz grabbed a pocketbook shoving her flip - flops inside. As Shelby turned to the door Mr. Dade stopped them. "Wait a minute." Shelby thought maybe he had second thoughts, as did Liz, her eyes conveying her anxiety. Mr. Dade walked out of the room. Liz shrugged her shoulders silently telling Shelby she had no idea what was up. Mr. Dade returned and handed Liz a wad of cash.

"You're a good daughter, Liz. Buy yourself something pretty for tonight. Your ma would want that."

Oh, Pop! Thanks." Liz threw her arms around her dad and squeezed him tight. He chuckled. "Go have fun, but not too long you have a big night ahead of you."

The girls grabbed each other's arms and giggled as they raced to the car.

First stop was to the hospital. Grace hadn't wanted to tell Jed but she wanted to make sure it was ok to get a manicure. Fortunately the Doctor that had administered care to Grace was on duty. He gave her a once over and said the manicure would be fine and he gave her antibacterial wipes to use afterwards. He also took the stitches out of her hair and said she could wash it completely now.

The girl's second stop was at Macy's. Shelby bought a pretty dress that she thought would be perfect for tonight. Shelby and her Mom helped Liz pick out an outfit as well. The next stop was to a Country Western store. Liz bought a beautiful pair of black cowboy boots. She was planning on wearing them tonight. Shelby bought a sexy pair of ankle boots with high heels that had the look of cowboy boots. They matched her new dress perfectly.

Next stop was to Grace's hair salon where she had her hair washed and blown out. While they were waiting Liz and Shelby glanced through the hair magazines. Shelby realized that Liz was eyeing up a new style but was nervous about it.

"You want a different hairstyle, Liz?"

"I've had my hair like this for as long

as I can remember."

"Do you want to change it?"

"Yes, yes, I really do. Nothing drastic, just different."

"Let's see if someone can do it now then." Shelby said as she headed to the receptionist desk. Another hairstylist could take Liz right away so Shelby helped Liz with describing what she envisioned. The hairstylists cut away a good portion of Liz's hair and bagged it for locks of love. She then gave Liz a beautiful, feminine cut that fell shoulder length with a sweeping side part bang that accentuated her high cheekbones and beautiful brown eyes. Liz looked stunning. She looked more mature, confident and her eyes sparkled.

The final stop was getting the manicures and pedicures. The girls talked about the upcoming evening. Liz was excited to be going. Lars had told Larry on the ride home from the after Christmas party that he liked Liz, like in a boyfriend way. Liz said it was a little tense at first, especially since Larry knew of all of Lars' previous escapades, but Lars had assured him he was serious. They had not told Liz's dad yet.

Liz asked about Clay and Shelby told her she really liked him. He was different than other guys she knew. She told Liz that they were going to keep in touch when she went back to Jersey but if either of them wanted to date, they could.

Shelby dropped Liz off and told her she'd see her that night. Liz ran in to the house, excited to show her dad and Larry her new haircut and her new boots. When Shelby and her Mom drove into the driveway Jed flew out the door to greet them. He noticed her hair immediately and before he could chastise her she told him they had stopped at the hospital and gotten her stitches taken out first. Shelby was grinning as she thought of how Jed took such good care of her Mom. Shelby was seriously happy for her, for them.

Chapter 7

Shelby put on a final spritz of perfume and twirled in the full mirror behind the bedroom door. She picked up her clutch and walked down the steps to the living area. The first sound she heard as she appeared on the last step, was Jed letting out a, "Wow."

Shelby looked across the room to Clay who was leaning against the kitchen counter drinking a soda. Clay looked up and felt his breath rush out of his lungs while his chest tightened. His cock swelled slightly and he quickly adjusted himself.

"Shelby, honey," said her Mom. "You look wonderful."

Clay walked out from behind the counter. He couldn't take his eyes off her. She wore a bronze dress with cap sleeves and a low scoop neck. The dress was A - line cut and she embellished it with a thin bronze belt. It accentuated her small curvy body perfectly. When she walked the skirt swirled seductively around her thighs. Clay looked her over head to toe. When he got to her shoes he stared at them and then slowly looked up to her face with a Cheshire cat grin. Her shoes were kick ass sexy and Shelby knew exactly what Clay was thinking.

"Damn Shelby, I'll be beating the guys back with a stick." Clay said. "You look fantastic."

"Thank you. You look pretty good yourself big guy." He did too. Shelby noticed he wore a nice pair of black jeans, black dress cowboy boots and a white button down shirt. He looked hot. Shelby's stomach was bumping with butterflies. Clay got Shelby's wrap and the two of them said good - bye to their parents and headed for the Elks.

The Elks parking lot was packed. Clay had told Shelby that pretty much everyone went the Elks on New Years Eve, young and old alike. Clay helped Shelby from the truck and they made their way inside. It was decorated with balloons and silver disco balls and Happy 2013 banners. There were table's set up around a large dance floor and a band played on a small stage that had the place jumping.

Clay found Ricky at a table with some other friends. They had saved two seats for them. Clay took Shelby's wrap to the coatroom and returned with two beers. Shelby sat back and watched the people dancing as Clay and Ricky talked. A slow song came on and Clay asked Shelby to dance. They molded together on the dance floor. Clay had to clench his fist to stop himself from reaching down to cup her ass. Shelby heard a squeal off to her side as Clays arm was ripped off from around her waist. A pretty girl spun Clay towards her and jumped into his arms. She wrapped her arms around his neck and kissed him all over his neck and face.

"Clay!" She squealed. "I have been calling you! Did you just get here?"

Shelby expected Clay to untangle himself from the girls embrace, considering what happened the last time someone had done this, but he didn't, instead, and much to Shelby's surprise. He picked up the girl and twirled her in a little circle.

"Dana when did you get back? Is your brother here too? I didn't know you'd called."

Shelby stood back trying to fight back the little green monster within. Clay finally remembered she was there. "Oh, hey Dana, I want you to meet Shelby. Her Mom is our new neighbor. She's visiting her. She's from Jersey."

"Hi." Said Dana giving her a once over that screamed competition. "I haven't seen this guy in ages. Mind if I take him for a spin?" Before Shelby could answer Dana had pulled Clay in tight and instead of Clay stopping her, he started laughing and twirled her on to the dance floor.

Shelby walked back to the table. She couldn't believe he just did that to her. Whenever she was introduced to a male, he quickly makes sure they know she was with him. But when she gets introduced to this red hair minx, she's, all of a sudden, the daughter of his neighbor. Shelby was seething. She mentally kicked herself for thinking he was different. Well she was leaving day after tomorrow. No need to become all unglued. She'd just distance herself and have a good time. Shelby looked around the room and spotted Liz and Lars at a table. Liz looked fabulous and Lars could barely take his eyes off her. When she approached the table Lars, Larry and the other men at the table rose. Shelby liked their manners.

"Hi, mind if I join you for a while?"

"That be great." Liz said.

Larry asked if he could get her a drink

and she said yes, so he excused himself from the table.

Shelby noticed that the song had stopped and another slow one was playing. Clay and Dana continued to dance. Her hands were all over him and they were laughing together. Liz noticed where Shelby was looking.

"Dana and Clay went all through school together. They have been best friends forever." Shelby looked at Liz like she just grew another head.

Liz continued. "Well she's one of his really close friends. As far as I know they've never dated."

"She doesn't live here anymore?" Shelby asked as she watched them.

"Nope, she and her brother, Dave moved to New York City last year."

"They look close." Shelby murmured.

"Yea I suppose they are, you okay?"

"Sure, hey how did your dad like your hair?'

"Oh Shelby, he almost cried. He said I looked just like my Mom."

Lars rubbed his hand gently on Liz's shoulders so she faced him.

"Babe, you want to dance?"

Liz looked torn; she didn't want to leave Shelby alone. One of the other guys at the table noticed this and jumped to the rescue.

"Shelby right? Would you care to dance with me?"

"That be nice." Shelby took the handsome man's hand as he led her to the dance floor. They started dancing and entered into a comfortable conversation.

"My name is Mac well everyone calls me Mac my last names MacPherson. My real name is Ken, but I like Mac"

"Well okay Mac it is. My name is Shelby, Shelby Jensen."

"And where are you from Shelby, Shelby Jensen?"

Shelby laughed.

"New Jersey, my Mom moved here this summer so I'm out for a visit."

"Well it's very nice to meet you. Did you come here alone? I have to say I'd be shocked that someone as pretty as you isn't already attached."

"I came with my Mom's neighbor, Clay Jones." She nodded towards Clay as he and Dana continued to dance and laugh.

"Oh, Clay huh. Should we be dancing?"

"Your kidding right?" Shelby dropped her hands from his shoulders and he grabbed them and put them back on his shoulders.

"You're right, he's dancing. I'm sorry."

So what do you do for living Mac?"

"I'm a lawyer."

"Really no cowboy, ranching anything?"

Mac laughed.

"Well will you think less of me if I tell you my specialty is in cattle and bull sales?"

Now Shelby laughed. "Really there's an actual need for that?"

Mac smiled down at her. He was a really handsome, thick blond hair and cobalt blue eyes. He was big in every way. She thought he was even larger than Lars. Shelby could tell just by touching him he was all muscle. She secretly wondered what the hell was in the mountain air that bred such huge, good-looking men. He didn't make her heart thud like Clay did but he was kind and interesting and Shelby soon began to relax and enjoy herself.

"What do you do?" He asked.

"I'm a teacher and a coach."

They both talked about their respective jobs and when the long montage of slow songs ended a fast one that Shelby like started up. Mac asked if she wanted to stay on the floor and she said yes. Mac was a really good dancer and he and Shelby soon had people turning their heads to watch them.

When the music turned to a fast song Clay realized he had been so wrapped up in talking to Dana that he'd forgotten about Shelby. He told Dana he needed to find Shelby and he headed back to his table. Dana stayed with him. When he got to the table he noticed Shelby wasn't there. He asked Ricky if he knew where she was. Rick just nodded to the dance floor. Clay turned towards where Ricky had nodded to see Shelby with Mac tearing up the dance floor. People were watching them. They moved well together and they were smiling and laughing. Mac had his hands encasing her hips as they synchronized their moves to the delight of the watching crowd. Clay felt nauseas. He knew Mac from school. Mac was a few years older than himself. He came from a wealthy family and he practiced law. He had been a hell of an athlete and played with Lars at Oregon. Clay took a step towards the dance floor. Two sets of hands gripped him holding him back.

Ricky had one arm and Dana had the other. "Looks like your little neighbor friend has found someone else to hang with." Dana said as she continued to hold his hand. One of Dana's friends saw Dana and grabbed her into a hug freeing Clay's hand. Clay turned to Ricky. Ricky looked at him and shook his head.

"What?" Clay said.

"You have to ask? I just thought you were really into Shelby."

"I am."

"Yea, I guess into her meaning like how you are with all your girls, easy come easy go."

"No you know it's different, I told you how I felt about her. She's different, special."

"I don't think so Clay. Sorry man. You dropped Shelby like a hot potato on the dance floor. I saw how you left her hanging there while you and Dana danced off."

"I just hadn't seen Dana in so long."

Dana was still engrossed in a conversation with her girl friends oblivious to Clay and Ricky's conversation.

"You better get your shit together man. First of all I think, and I said this to you years ago. Dana likes you more than just a friend. You didn't dance like 'just friends.'"

"Shit." Clay said. "What do I do?"

"Well which girl do you like?"

Clay looked from Shelby to Dana and back to Shelby.

"I'll always care for Dana, but Shelby, Shelby, she could be special, scratch that, she is special."

"Well my friend, you may have seriously fucked that up."

Ricky nodded back to the dance floor where a slow song had started again and Shelby and Mac stayed on the floor.

After the slow song ended Mac walked Shelby back to their table. He rested his hand lightly on the small of her back as he guided her back. Shelby dropped into her seat laughing. Everyone at the table complimented her and Mac on how well they danced together. Mac, instead of sitting back in his original chair, took one from another table and placed it next to Shelby. Clay watched with trepidation. His gut hurt. Dana grabbed Clay's hand and tried to guide him to her table. Clay shook off her hand.

"Dana, I'm here with someone."

"Oh Clay she's already being taken care of honey. Hang with me."

Clay realized he didn't want to hang with Dana. He wanted to be with Shelby, his beautiful Shelby, and now because he had gotten caught up with seeing his childhood friend and forgotten her. Shit, he really had forgotten her. How could he do that?

"No Dana, thank you, you go hang with your friends."

"Clay, you're being silly. That girl is happy with Mac. Look at them."

Clay looked back at the table. Mac had his arm draped lazily over Shelby's chair. He wasn't touching her though. Shelby was busy chatting with Liz and Lars. Clay shook his head. He didn't know what to do. Mac was a good guy. Clay didn't want any trouble with him, plus Mac was a big dude. If they fought, it wouldn't be pretty.

"Come on Clay." Dana tugged on his hand again.

"No." Clay tugged his hand away from hers. Clay saw Shelby watching him. Shit she saw Dana holding his hand. "Well suit yourself Clay. Hopefully I'll be near you at midnight." She kissed him on the cheek and walked away.

Clay took a step towards the table where Shelby was sitting. Ricky placed his hand on his arm again. "You cool man. It's Mac."

"Yea, I'm cool."

Clay walked over to the table where Shelby was sitting and said hello to everyone. He looked at Liz and saw how she was glowing under the unfettered attention Lars was giving her. He should have been doing that with Shelby.

"Hi." Clay said to the table. He wasn't sure of the reception he'd get.

The table said hello and Larry invited him to sit in Mac's old seat on the other side of the table. The table was talking football, of course. Shelby was wrapped up in the conversation and wowing the men with her knowledge of the game. Clay watched Mac sitting next to Shelby. He started a silent mantra to himself, 'don't touch her, please, don't touch her.'

Shelby finally looked up to him. She'd been avoiding his eyes. Clay looked at her hoping to convey to her a silent plea of 'I'm sorry'. Shelby pulled her eyes away. Clay sucked in a tight breath. This was not good. Lars and Liz got up to dance a slow song and before Mac could ask Shelby to dance, Clay stood up and said. "Shelby would you like to dance?" Mac looked over to Clay and then back to Shelby. He didn't look happy.

"No thanks Clay not right now." Clay cringed and sat back down. Mac had a little smile on his face that Clay wanted to wipe the floor with. "Actually, I need to use the rest room." Mac pulled his chair back to allow her to exit and stood up still displaying his impeccable manners. Shelby nodded a thank you to him.

Clay waited about a minute before he too excused himself. He walked towards the bathroom. He needed to get her to talk to him. He waited in the hallway outside the ladies room. The door finally opened and Dana stepped out, her eyes lite up when she saw Clay. Shelby stepped out right after her. Dana wrapped her hand around Clay's arm.

"Oh, Clay. Shelby and I just had the best talk. She knows how much I've missed you. She said she'd find her own way home so you can take me home tonight."

"What?!"

Shelby put her eyes to the floor and started back to the main room.

"No fucking way!" Clay bit out rather loudly turning heads from those nearby.

Shelby turned around to face him. Clay was livid.

"Shelby said she'd be fine Clay honey." Dana put her hands on Clays chest and brought her body close to his. Clay pushed her hands off of his chest and stalked to Shelby. "Back off Dana." He bit out. Dana shrank back against the wall as if she'd been slapped.

"Shelby don't even think about stepping into that room." Clay said barely reigning in his anger. "We need to talk."

"No Clay we don't. I'm just a neighbor. Isn't that how you introduced me to Dana? Funny how you don't introduce me like that to men. I'm only here for another day. Dana really likes you. She has for a long time. Tell him Dana. Tell him!" Shelby was trying to remain composed. She was livid and did not need this shit!

"Clay, I'm sorry. I do. I have for awhile." Dana's bottom lip was quivering.

Shelby walked back past Clay and put her arm around Dana glaring up at Clay.

Clay sighed loudly. "Shit. Dana we've been friends forever. Great friends, you're one of my best. But I don't like you like that." Dana had tears rolling down her face.

"Clay," Shelby said." Maybe you like her more than you think you do. You know like Lars realizing how he really liked Liz."

"What? Shelby, no I don't. I care for Dana like a brother would a sister. Why would you say that?"

Shelby didn't answer him, just

continued to comfort Dana. Why would Shelby think that? Clay was racking his brain. Dana excused herself and went back in to the bathroom. Shelby started back towards the main room. Clay grabbed her arm before she made it.

"Leave me alone Clay. I'm not with you tonight. You made it perfectly clear how you feel about me."

"Shelby, no, I'm sorry. I fucked up. I know I did. Please lets go talk."

Mac, Liz and Lars chose that time to walk into the hall.

"Everything okay back here?" Mac said.

"Yes, Mac, thank you. Everything is fine. Liz will you walk me back to the table please?" Shelby asked quietly.

"Sure, honey, come on." Lars gave Liz a little pat on the shoulder.

Liz turned her head and spoke over her shoulder. "You boys play nice okay." Then she shuttled Shelby back to the table.

"What's going on Clay?' Mac asked.

"I came with Shelby."

Lars grunted next to him. Mac stared down at Clay.

"So things change. You're with Dana now. I'll take Shelby home."

Clay almost launched himself at Mac right there. Dana came back out of the bathroom.

"Clay." She looked up at him with sad eyes. "Can we go talk, Please?"

Clay didn't know what to do. If he didn't go after Shelby he might lose her forever, if he hadn't already. If he didn't talk to Dana, he might lose a childhood friend, forever. Clay looked to Lars. Lars shrugged his shoulders. "Hey, man." Lars said. "I'm new to the dating game. You don't want advise from me."

"Clay please!" Dana tugged on his hand.

"Dana, I really have to talk to Shelby."

Mac and Lars left them and went into the men's room.

"Dana, I really like Shelby, I feel something so strong with her, well it's just different. I'm so sorry if that hurts your feelings. I care for you too, but like a sister. I've really hurt her."

Dana sniffed in her tears and sarcastically remarked. "Wow, you might really like her? Well, I might love you?"

"Please don't Dana. I need you in my life as a friend. We've been through so much."

Dana marched away as Lars and Mac

came out of the bathroom and Clay put his palm on Macs chest to stop him from entering the main room. Mac looked down at the extended hand, then to Clay, then to Lars. He did not look happy.

"I really like her Mac."

"You have a crappy way of showing it my man." Clay lowered his arm.

"Major fuck up on my part. She's her own woman. Just want you to know, if you make a play for her I'll be right next to you. And if you hurt her in any little way, you'll answer to me."

"Clay you're the one who hurt her. Maybe I should make you answer to me."

The tension in the hallway rose to an uncomfortable level. Lars didn't think he should leave but he thought it best to get Shelby and let her calm these men down. He walked back to the table where he found Liz and her in a quiet conversation.

"Shelby, you might want to douse the fire between Clay and Mac or there will be blood."

Liz and Lars followed Shelby back to the hallway. "What's going on?" Shelby said.

Mac and Clay had been having a heated discussion, of that, she was sure.

"Shelby," Mac started, "I've known you for a little over an hour and I know I'd like to see you again." Clay sucked in a deep breath and his eyes turned dark with emotion. Shelby had seen those eyes back in the biker bar. "But this guy claims to really care for you, and I've known him most of my life. He's a good guy, but he's a player. The thing is I think he's serious, about you I mean." Clay swung his head towards Mac. What was he saying? "I'm here for the night and if by any slim chance you feel half as strongly about me, as I feel about you, well then we can just see where that goes. Thing is, I do believe this man really likes you in a special way." He nodded at Clay. " So if you do care for him. You might want to hear him out."

Mac gave Shelby a kiss on her check and motioned for Lars and Liz to follow him. Clay looked at Shelby. She couldn't look him in the eyes. He knew that wasn't good. "Shelby, please look at me." Shelby looked up after a long pause.

"Baby, I'm so sorry."

Shelby didn't say anything. She stared into Clays eyes. She wished she could read minds. She was so confused.

"Shelby, Dana is a childhood friend. I told her she is only a friend. I don't want more with her. I want more ...with you."

Shelby looked to the floor and then back up to Clay. "You really hurt me Clay. I'm only here for another day. There's no reason to throw something with Dana away."

"I know I hurt you. I don't know why I introduced you to Dana the way I did. I just was so surprised to see her."

"Maybe it's a mind slip. Maybe you meant to introduce me that way because you unconsciously didn't want Dana to think of me as... As...Something more."

"No, it's not that. God I'm so sorry. Shelby. I think I may be falling for you, I can't believe it myself how much I care for you. I told Dana. I told Mac and Lars. Shelby this is so not how I thought tonight would go."

Clay ran his hands through his black hair. He leaned back against the wall behind him.

"How did you want this night to go?" Shelby asked quietly.

Clay pushed off the wall and moved to Shelby. She took a step back from him. Clay frowned. "Will you come sit down and let me tell you?" Shelby nodded and they entered the main room again. Clay found a table in the far end of the room away from the band. Shelby caught eyes with Liz as they walked through the hall. Liz gave her a thumb up sign. Shelby laughed when mac gave her one too. He was a good guy and it made Shelby smile as she walked with Clay. Clay pulled the chair out for her and then he moved his chair so he was right next to hers. Clay took her hands that were on the table within his.

"I wanted to dance with you, just you all night. I wanted to introduce you to everyone as my girl. I wanted to touch you all night long. Little touches that would make you want me, make you need me." Shelby sighed and her eyes rimmed with emotional tears. Clay touched her soul like no one had ever before.

"I wanted to steal kisses throughout the night, some short, some so long and hot that we'd think about leaving, but we wouldn't"

Someone shouted and the room began

a count down from 20 to midnight. Clay stood and pulled Shelby up with him. He wrapped his arms around her.

"At midnight we'd be on the dance floor."

The countdown had reached 5...4...3...2...1 and the place erupted around them. Except neither Clay nor Shelby heard any of it.

"And I would kiss you so deeply we'd almost forget to breath. Then I would lean in to you and whisper, that I'm falling in love with you Shelby Jensen." Clay cupped the sides of her face with his hands and looked into her eyes with such intensity that Shelby almost did forget to breath.

"I'm not giving up on us because you're leaving. We have some connection that I've never felt before with anyone. I care for you too much to let you slide through my life without trying." Clay looked into Shelby's eyes praying she'd see his sincerity.

"That's how I wanted our night to go." Clay whispered to her. He bent his head to her and found her lips. He kissed her softly coaxing her lips open so he could stroke her with his tongue, Shelby reached up and wrapped her arms around his neck pulling him closer. Shelby's heart began to beat back to life.

"Shelby please forgive me, please don't give up on me." He kissed her again and then rested his forehead against hers.

"It's been a week, a short week. How can you know? Falling... really?"

"I feel what I feel Shel's. I know it's only been a week. When I saw you with Mac my heart almost stopped."

"Clay maybe you just are reacting to seeing me with another guy?"

"No baby, it's not. I've been feeling this way, shit since playing football with you."

"I don't know. It's too fast and I'm

leaving."

"I know. I am so sorry I danced with her Shelby. I just forgot. I wasn't thinking."

"That's just it Clay, you forgot. You saw Dana and I became secondary. I'm not sure how to feel right now."

"What do you mean? About me? About us? Dana? What?"

"Everything Clay. You introduce me as a neighbor. You forget about me, leave me on the dance floor, and dance for at least 15 minutes without even a care as to where I am. Your friend, who's a girl tells me, in the bathroom she's so glad we're just neighbors because she's in love with you. Then someone pays attention to me and all of a sudden you really care for me."

Clay was visibly shaken with Shelby's words. "Wow, when you say it like that."

"Like that, cause it's how it was."

"Fuck me." Clay drew one hand through his hair. Shelby realized this was one of his stress tells.

Shelby took Clay by the hand. "How about we just try to salvage the night?"

"Can we?"

"We'll find out." Shelby grabbed his other hand and led him on to the dance floor. The high - spirited celebration continued for another hour before people started to head home. Liz, Lars, Larry and Mac all kissed Shelby Happy New Years before they left. Mac gave Shelby a sweet smile and slipped her his business card as he whispered 'just in case.' in her ear. Lars wouldn't let Liz kiss anyone except Shelby which Shelby thought was sweet. Ricky found them on the dance floor and draped his arm around both of them so they were a threesome slow dancing.

"Ricky tell Shelby what I was going to tell her tonight."

"That you were falling hard for her, and you might even love her." Ricky was a little tipsy and Shelby smiled at how cute he was acting.

"You know we have to take him home, right?" Shelby said to Clay.

"I know."

The evening ended with no more drama. Clay had been attentive to her the rest of the evening but the damage was done. Shelby cared for him. He made her feel things that she had never felt. But he'd also made her feel things she had felt before, betrayal, uncertainty, and insecurity. She knew he was definitely sorry for what he'd done. He was quieter than usual and Shelby missed the confident cowboy that awakened her sensual side.

Chapter 8

They dropped Ricky off and headed back home. Clay pulled off on to the side of the driveway and turned to Shelby. He unhooked his seatbelt and scooted over to her. He wasn't sure if she'd accept him. He was like a teenager wanting a first kiss. He unhooked Shelby's seatbelt and lifted her so she was cradled in his lap; his left arm supported her back. He kept waiting for her to shut him down, she didn't.

"I wish the night had gone differently and I know this is all on me, but I'm praying you can forgive me. I have one more day with you, one short day to show you how good we are together."

Shelby took her left hand and caressed his cheek with her fingers before resting her palm there. "I care for you Clay, so much.

That's why tonight was so hard. I do forgive you; it's the forgetting that's difficult. I don't know what's in our future. I do know that I could have been with Mac tonight. It's nice to feel wanted." She felt Clay tense up underneath her. "But he didn't make my insides jump like you do. He didn't make my heart squeeze, like you do. He didn't take my breath away, like you do. I didn't want to kiss him... Forever, like I do with you." Shelby felt Clay harden beneath her. He bent down to her and kissed so tenderly she moaned into his mouth.

He continued to kiss her and she tangled her fingers in his thick hair. The windows fogged and neither of them even noticed. Clay was rubbing her bare leg that was draped over his thighs. His hand moved slowly upwards and Shelby felt her nether lips become moist. Clay reached her thong and cupped her mound feeling her heated response. He groaned. He took his thumb and pulled the little elastic to one side then he slowly drew circles around her clit until

Shelby was writhing on top of his lap.

"Clay." She panted. "Don't tease."

"I want you Shel's. I want to be buried so deep inside you tonight. Is that going to happen?"

"Yes, that's going to happen."

"Pinky swear?" Clay teased using one of Shelby's favorite expressions.

"Pinky swear, Oh my God Clay, yes. Pinky swear."

Clay used three finger pads and rubbed them aggressively over Shelby's clit. She exploded on the spot. He drew her orgasm out and still didn't stop. He worked her hard until she felt the prickle of another orgasm start to take hold. Clay knew when she was teetering again by how her body was reacting. He took his hand away from her sensitive folds and Shelby groaned in frustration. He picked Shelby up and placed her back in her seat and buckled her in. She looked at him frustrated. He had primed her and left her hanging. Clay gave her a quick kiss on the nose.

"I'll finish you baby. In my bed."

Chapter 9

Clay hopped out of the truck quickly so he could help Shelby down from the cab. Before she could put her feet on the ground Clay lifted her over his shoulder in a fireman's carry. He placed his hand firmly on her bare thonged ass.

"God, I have been wanting to touch you here all night." Clay said huskily.

Shelby laughed and wiggled trying to get Clay to put her down but Clay held her legs firmly with one hand while his other hand lay possessively on her ass. When they entered the house. The living room was quiet except for the crackle of the dying fire in the stone fireplace. Clay lowered Shelby gently and she slid seductively over his front. Shelby felt his thick cock through his jeans and shivered with lusty anticipation. Clay took Shelby's hand within his and headed towards the stairs.

Shelby took a step with him then drew up short, keeping her hand in his forcing him to stop walking. Clay looked down at Shelby wondering why she stopped them. Shelby looked at Clay, then at the bear hide rug in front of the low fire, then back to Clay again.

"Clay would you make love to me on the rug, in front of the fire?"

Clay's heart seized with unchecked emotion. How she could still desire him after what he had done to her tonight was a miracle. He'd been so worried. Clay couldn't talk without betraying his emotion. Shelby continued to look at him with her hooded baby blue eyes. She opened her mouth, "Pl......" but Clay put a finger on her lips to hush her.

"Sweetheart..." Clays voice was trembling. "I will hold you, kiss you, make love to you any where, anytime. You never,

ever, have to ask twice. I think I will always want you Shelby, always."

Shelby's eyes filled with tears with Clays heartfelt words. He brushed a tear away from her cheek and kissed where it had been. Shelby reached up and forcefully pulled Clay down to her. Their mouths met with a hunger that bordered starvation. Clay groaned as she ground her stomach into his length. He was marble hard and his cock begged to be released from his confining jeans. Shelby reached between their bodies and rubbed her palm along the beckoning bulge. Clay snapped his head back and practically growled.

Clay stepped back from Shelby. He let out a raged breath holding Shelby at arms length with his hands on her shoulders. He took another step back and turned away from Shelby moving towards the kitchen. 'He cannot be hungry now.' Shelby thought. She squeezed her legs together to dull the throbbing he had set in motion. Clay grabbed a kitchen chair and positioned it at the bottom of the stairs.

Clay walked back to Shelby and put his hands back on her shoulders. "It's a signal I have with my Dad. If the chair is there it means don't come down to the living room."

Shelby nodded then frowned. Clay picked up her signals. He knew her, he knew her probably better than she knew herself.

"We've both had woman here honey." Shelby nodded again. Clay tipped her chin up so she was looking into his eyes.

"Never upstairs though. I've never had anyone one in my room, except you." Shelby pulled Clay to her and buried her face in his chest. She drank in his woody essence. She loved how he smelled. He didn't wear cologne. He had a clean scent that made her want to lick him head to toe.

"Shelby, I have one request."

Shelby looked up at him as she rubbed her hands on his back, massaging the hard planes of his athletic build.

"Will you keep your shoes on please?"

Shelby beamed up at him. She knew these shoes were perfect! Clay returned her smile and she nodded that she would indeed fuck him with her shoes on. Slowly they undressed each other in front of the smoldering fire. The room was dark except for what light was coming from the hearth. Their bodies pressed together once divested of all their clothes, except for Shelby's heels.

Clay helped Shelby to lie down on her back on the bear hide. He lay next to her running his hand all over her soft skin. Shelby was looking up at Clay while he alternated his gaze between her liquid eyes and her curvaceous body. The moment was pristine, precious, soul barrenly sweet.

"I've never felt this way about anyone before Shel's. I know I have to earn back your trust. I will. I swear I will."

Shelby didn't respond. She had been falling for him, hard. She'd been so close, but tonight had reminded Shelby to keep a tight leash on her feelings. It was simply self-preservation. Yet, he made her feel things she had never felt either. She traced Clay's jaw line with her finger then moved to caress his lips. He pulled her finger into his mouth and gently suckled it, before leaning down to kiss her. He knew her silence was her processing what he'd said. Clay needed time. Time to earn back her trust. Time to show her he was serious about her. Time he was quickly running out of.

Clay kissed his way down her body. He cupped her breasts and licked around her nipples until they were tight and shivering. He gently nipped one causing Shelby to inhale sharply. Clay looked up at her never taking his lips from her. She was glorious. Her hair was fanned out around her head. Her eyes were closed and her thick lashes kissed her face. Her delectable pink lips were set creating a small O shape. She moaned softly under his skillful touches. Her breaths were heavy and he hadn't even touched her below the waist yet. Clay slid himself lower blazing a searing trail with his wicked tongue until he was even with her mound. Her lips were glistening. She opened her thighs wider almost brazenly inviting him in. Clay blew on her hidden jewel and she groaned grasping his hair in frustration.

"I got you baby." Clay whispered up to her.

He licked her wet folds and relished her sweet taste. He could go down on her all day. Her juices alone could feed him. Clay had to put his forearms over Shelby's hips to stop her from moving. He was going to love her all night long, but this first time he was going to take his time. Clay suckled her tiny pearl and drew his tongue over it in a back forth motion. Shelby was coming apart.

"Clay, Oh God, Clay... Clay please, Clay I'm so close."

Clay took his thumbs and pulled her pink folds apart for better access. He buried his face into her stretched lips and open mouth tongued her. Shelby's body was already bowed. Clay grazed his teeth over her clit and she imploded. She called out his name and thrashed her head with the intensity of the climax. Her core quivered violently as Clay drew out her orgasm. Shelby couldn't stop coming. He flat tongue licked her over another edge and she saw black spots. Shelby was as close to passing out as she had ever been. She realized she had Clays hair in a death grip and relaxed her hold on him. Clay peered up at her keeping his face between her thighs, giving her tiny licks that caused her pelvis to buck upon contact. Shelby pulled Clays hair so he would come back up to her.

Clay slowly kissed his way back up her body. He knew he had just given her two powerful orgasms. He didn't care that he hadn't come. He was so hard, so turned on; he would explode with a simple touch. All he cared about was showing Shelby how much he cared about her, that she meant more to him than anything he'd ever had before. Shelby pulled Clay up to her. She grasped his face between her hands and made him meet her eyes.

Shelby spoke softly to him as she looked into his green eyes. "You are a wonderful lover Clay."

Clay didn't answer, he simply dipped his head and sweetly brushed his lips against hers.

"Make love to me Clay. I want you in me. I need you. I need to feel you inside me."

Clay smiled at Shelby with almost a sad smile. He needed Shelby too and when she said she wanted him he felt a flutter of hope return. Clay knew she was wet and needed no more foreplay. He used his knees to push her thighs further apart. Then he reached under her body to grasp her ass.

Clay braced her small body holding it still and slid inside her balls deep. He adjusted his hips to sink further in pulling up on her hips for even more access. His final adjustment made him hiss with satisfaction. He allowed himself a moment to compose his physical and emotional state. He loved how he was planted so deeply inside of her. Shelby groaned her approval with their current position. Clay placed his hands on the rug and used his arms to push Shelby's knees up. Her thighs were pressed back towards her chest and her knees dangled over his arms. Her 'fuck me' shoes dangled over his arms outside of his elbows. She was fully exposed and Clay controlled the tempo.

Slowly he started to press in and out of her. He pushed so deeply inside of Shelby she gasped at the intense pressure. Clay found her eyes with his.

"You okay?"

"You're so deep Clay, God you are so deep. It feels so good. You feel so good."

Clay didn't need more encouragement. He increased his pace driving into her, rotating his hips so he reached all her sweet spots. Shelby was quaking underneath him. She couldn't move her hips but she bore down on his cock with her vaginal walls massaging Clays pounding cock. He felt his balls tighten and knew he was going to erupt like never before.

"Shelby, are you close, baby? I'm close I want us to come together."

"Oh God, yes Clay, yes." Clay took one hand and rubbed his fingers against her distended clit. Shelby bucked uncontrollably as she climaxed violently. Clay shot his semen deep. He growled as his climax shook the breath from him. Clay collapsed on top of Shelby, trying to keep his weight off her. Shelby's eyes were closed and her head was tilted to the side, she had hazed out.

Clay slid to her side and caressed her face. "Shelby, baby. Come back to me baby." Shelby's eyes fluttered and she sucked in a breath.

"Oh, my God Clay. That was unbelievable. You made me see spots. I remember, I remember the intensity of... You know... Then I... Sort of blacked out."

"I know sweetheart. You okay now?"

Shelby reached up and ran her hand over her face.

"I'm okay. I can't move yet." She giggled shyly.

"You don't need to honey. I'll take care of you."

Clay stood up, moved the chair back to the kitchen table and gathered their clothes. He laid their clothes on Shelby's stomach so she grasped them with her hands. Clay then bent down and lifted Shelby into his arms. He carried her up the stairs and into his room. Clay gently laid Shelby down on his bed, took off her awesome, 'fuck me' shoes, and went to get a washcloth. He gently washed her, then dried her and pulled the covers up over her hips. Clay returned to the bathroom washed himself then returned to his room. He slipped under the covers with Shelby and drew her to him. She snuggled into his waiting arms and rested her head on his shoulder.

"I could fall in love with you Clay." Shelby said so softly he almost heard her. He didn't think she knew she was speaking the words out loud. "I could love you so easily."

Clay stroked her arm and held her to him. He thought about the time he had wasted tonight. Time he could have been holding, loving her. Clay kissed the top of Shelby's head. She was already asleep.

Chapter 10

They made love again during the night. They didn't speak. Clay caressed her and Shelby responded. They touched and kissed and Clay rode her until they climaxed together before falling back to sleep, entwined. They needed to feel each other.

Shelby stirred next to Clay. Clay was partially draped over Shelby's back. His cock was somehow hard even though he had used it through the night. Clay reached under Shelby's legs and played with her clit. Her arousal from her sleep was secondary to the arousal she now felt humming through her body. Clay reached under Shelby's and pulled her to her knees. He made sure she was sufficiently wet and then he entered her from behind. Clay glided in and out of her setting a pattern of slow then fast. Shelby would meet his push in by grinding back on his cock. He took one hand and started to twist her nipples that were swinging from the rocking motion and then he took his other hand and moved it to the front of Shelby's mound circling but not touching her pearly bud. Shelby started to moan her pleasure and Clay was panting. Wanting Shelby to climax was priority number one so Clay changed the rhythm of his pumps so he was now banging her with hard forceful thrusts. He attacked her clit with fervor and twisted and pinched her sensitive nipples. Shelby threw her face into the pillow and screamed his name as a violent orgasm crashed through her overly stimulated body. Knowing Clay hadn't climaxed yet, Shelby reached underneath her open legs and grasped Clays heavy twin sacks. She rolled them in her warm hand sending Clay into a frenzied orgasm that left him so muscle less that he dropped on top of Shelby's spent body with a groan.   They lay together breathing deeply, regain their senses.

"Clay, what time is it?" Clay

reluctantly opened his eyes to glance at the clock.

"It's 11:15."

"Oh, wow we really slept."

Clay chuckled. "We didn't sleep all that much baby."

Shelby still hadn't opened her eyes. She gently swatted his leg that was straddling her hip.

"We have to get up." She said.

"Why?"

"Clay, this is my favorite TV day of the year. Football, all day. I don't want to miss anything."

"Ummm, my kind of woman." Clay murmured groggily.

Shelby dragged her self out from under Clay's warm body. She needed to use the bathroom. She looked around the room and saw a tee shirt lying on a chair. She pulled it over her head and went to the door. Clay got out of bed. Shelby cast him an appreciative glance. His body was honed and magnificent. If she were a sculpture she'd choose him for a model. Shelby opened the door and because she was busy appreciating Clay's body didn't see Jed who was walking down the hall.

Jed saw the little pixie of a girl come out from his son's room. He saw she wore his tee shirt and that it hung to her thighs. Her hair was mussed and her lips were plump from use. Shelby looked up and saw him before they collided. Jed colored, as did Shelby. Clay watched the exchange from his room.

"Quid pro quo, Jed." Shelby giggled as she hurried on to the bathroom.

"Geez, just like her mother." Jed muttered. Clay smiled and just shrugged his shoulders. His dad reached and shut the door. He didn't need Grace seeing this.

Clay and Shelby showered and dressed for the New Years day. They were staying home and watching football all day. Clays aunt Betty and uncle Josh were coming over also. Clay could take Shelby over to his friend's house, but he had no desire to share her with anyone. Plus she wanted to be with her Mom on her last day. Clay also didn't want to run into Dana. He hoped she had processed what he had said and they could remain friends.

Shelby was relaxed, sated. Clay had loved her so well last night. She sat on the ottoman paired with Clay's chair. Her back was snuggled up to Clay's chest and her head rested on him. She didn't care that Betty and her Mom had given them the raised eyebrow before masking their faces. Shelby needed Clay's contact. She was leaving and she was already feeling the unpleasant pull that would be all encompassing when she left.

Clay ran his hands leisurely up and down Shelby's arms. He knew their open display of affection was causing a little stir among his family and Grace but he didn't care. He didn't care at all. He knew Shelby wanted to spend the time with her Mom but if he could, he would carry her back upstairs and make love to her again and again. His cock semi'd as he thought of being buried inside her tight welcoming sheath. Shelby felt him harden on her lower back. She placed her hands on his legs and gave him a squeeze. He looked down at her. She took his breath away. Clay took some deep breaths to steady his thoughts and regain control of his body.

Shelby wanted to kiss Clay right then. She was glad she wasn't a male because her desire would not be as hidden as it was now. She was wet and her nipples had pebbled. One sexy look from Clay sent her into hyper arousal mode. Shelby stretched and looked over her shoulder at Clay.

"Anyone want to take a walk?" Shelby asked the room. It was halftime so it wasn't too obvious. She only hoped Clay would be the only one taking her up on the offer.

Clay chimed in with a quick yes and stood after Shelby did to get their coats. Grace started to rise. "That sounds good, a little fresh air." Shelby and Clay were quick to mask their disappointment. "Jed?" Grace asked looking at her handsome man. They were sitting on the couch and Jed's arm was lovingly drawn over her shoulder keeping her close. Jed leaned down and whispered something to Grace and she smiled up to him with a gentle, loving smile.

"No sweetheart, stay here with me okay?" Clay could have hugged his dad if it wouldn't have been so obvious. Grace nodded her answer and snuggled deeper into her handsome man's arms.

Clay helped Shelby with her coat and they stepped out side into the frigid air. Clay took Shelby's gloved hand within his and they headed to the barn. Clay opened the side door and led Shelby inside. The ranch hands had a shortened day and had already finished their jobs. The barn was empty except for the animals. Shelby walked over to cat's box and knelt down to play with the tiny kittens. Clay took this time to check on one his prized bull at the far end stall. He had over 30 bulls that he personally took care of.

Shelby came to stand by him. "I've requested the 5 Star be considered as a PBR stock bull contractor."

"I didn't know that." Said Shelby.

"Yea, if we get picked, our bulls get contracted out for certain PBR events. It's a pretty big deal. If we get chosen it says something about the caliber of bulls we are raising here."

" How does that work, if you get chosen?"

" We are given certain events to send some of our bulls to. For each event we'd send about 8 bulls."

"Who goes with them?"

"We'd have to send someone."

"You?"

"I'd love that but with dad and football I couldn't leave the ranch. I'd send one of the hands, I guess."

Shelby turned into Clay and wrapped her arms around his waist. Clay pulled her so close. He took his gloves off and slid his fingers into her hair as he anchored her for his touch. Their lips met, tentatively at first. Their tongues stroked against each other and ignited the passion that had been barely held in check inside. Clay groaned their coats not allowing for the contact he craved.

"Shelby, I want you again, I want you now."

Shelby stepped away from leaving him rasping unevenly. She unzipped her coat and let it pool at her feet. She took off her gloves and unzipped her jeans slipping out of her Ugg boots then her jeans. Lastly she wiggled out of underwear. Clay was afraid to move. His cock was rock hard and Shelby's little strip tease had him a stroke away. This woman could ignite a wet match. Shelby reached for Clays jeans and unzipped them. He shrugged out of his coat and let that lay on the barn floor with Shelby's. He toed off his barn boots and Shelby pulled down his pants and boxers and guided him to step out of them. They had left their shirts on, it wasn't freezing in the barn, but it wasn't warm either. Clays thick cock stood bumping against his abdomen. It throbbed, pre-cum wept from his slit. Shelby saw his passion. She knelt before him and licked up his length. Clay growled and spread his legs for purchase. Shelby lapped him head to base. She traced his vein that ran underneath driving him wild. His hands were entwined in her hair but not pressuring her. Shelby suckled her way up to his smooth head. She swirled her tongue around the large plum shape moving the tip over her tongue to drive under his ridge with some pressure. Clay waiver on his feet.

"Shel's, Jesus, baby." He grunted out.

Shelby loved how he tasted. His size was impressive and she knew she couldn't take him fully so she worked him so he wouldn't even notice. Shelby wrapped her lips tightly around him and sucked him in as far as she could. She rhythmically dragged back to his head, sucking hard as she pulled back. When she got to his head she maneuver her tongue so it swirled around and then she tightened her lips again and traveled back down as far as she could go. Clay was delirious, he couldn't think, he could only feel. Shelby's lips and mouth were pulling him towards a mind - blowing climax. He reached back to hold the stall behind him. He was that unsteady. Shelby took her hands, which had been on his thighs and wrapped them both around his cock. Clay was so hung that she could wrap both her fists around his base and still have room for her mouth to bob up and down his shaft. Shelby moved her hands so that her right one moved counter clockwise then clockwise and her left moved clock wise then counter clockwise. She fisted him tightly as she continued twisted her hands and sucking greedily on his head down to her fists.

Clay was shaking. He was going to blow and he prayed he could remain on his feet. His balls constricted and Shelby felt him grow larger, tighten and then erupt sending warm cum down her throat, which she greedily sucked down. Clay groaned loudly and bucked into her mouth. He was still coming. His butt cheeks were clenched as he continued to fill Shelby's mouth with his seed. Shelby reached under his base and gently massaged his sacks wringing him dry. Clay fell back against the stall. His legs couldn't hold him any longer. Shelby kissed his wet head and stood up.

Clay couldn't talk. She had just sucked him speechless. She had given him not only the best blow- job, ever, but he swore he might have even come twice. Could guys do that? Shit, he didn't know but she had literally blown his mind. Shelby looked at him with an amused smile. She realized she had surpassed his expectations, and she loved that she had been able to surprise him.

Clay came off the stall still breathing hard and reached for Shelby. She stepped into his arms pressing her cheek against his chest.

"Shelby, that was unbelievable. You are unbelievable. Thank you."

Shelby hugged him relishing how good he felt. Clay bent down and picked up his coat and walked to three bales of stacked hay, where he placed his coat over the top bale. He led Shelby to the hay and helped her climb up top of them. Her knees were even with his chest and Clay pushed them wide open then placed them over his wide shoulders. He grinned devilishly at her and then dove in to her folds. He held her pink succulent lips open with his thumbs as his shoulders held her legs up and opened. Shelby keened above him. He steadied her with his forearms as he used his mouth to munch on her clit. Shelby grasped Clays hair and held on for fear of flying off the stacked bales of hay. Clay took one hand off her lips but used his finger and thumb of the other hand to continue to hold her open. He moved his free hand to her creamy core and slid two fingers into her tight hole. Shelby moaned and bucked forcing his mouth to press on her clit harder. Clay pumped his fingers inside of her. His fingers were drenched in her juices. He twisted his fingers and scissored them driving Shelby wild.

"Clay, oh God Clay, I'm so close." Clay took his fingers and moved them in a come hither motion that rubbed Shelby's G spot. He closed his mouth around her clit and sucked on it like a tit.

"Ohhhhh.... I'm coming..... Oh God..... I'm coming......." Shelby moaned as she bucked uncontrollably grounding her pussy against his face. Clay suckled her until she stopped bucking and withdrew his fingers. He brought his glistening fingers that had just been inside her to his mouth sucking them in. Shelby watched and bucked again as another small orgasm nipped her body. Shit, sucking her juices from his fingers had given her an orgasm. This woman was sexual. Shelby moaned and tried to squeeze her legs shuts but Clays shoulder still held her wide. Clay leaned back down and gave her lips a final short french kiss and stood up. He had a sweet grin on his face. He knew he had just returned the mind -blowing orgasm Shelby had given him back to her.

Shelby looked at Clay and felt her emotions crash in on her. Her eyes rimmed with tears and she started crying. Clay lifted her from the hay and pulled her in close.

"Baby, shhhh, Shelby, honey. It's going to be okay. It will baby." Clay knew she was thinking about them being separated. He knew she couldn't say it but she was as emotionally invested as he was. Clay stroked her back and her hair and let her cry it out. He hated for her to be hurting. Shelby brought her emotions under control, but she couldn't let Clay go. He sensed her needs as if they were his own and continued to gently hold her securely with in his strong arms.

Shelby had finally gathered herself and stood back.

"I'm sorry I let loose. I'm not usually such a baby." She wiped her face with the back of her hand.

"Shel's, I feel it too. My stomach is so twisted knowing you're leaving. One week, I've known you for one week and I know 'without you' is going to hurt."

Shelby pressed back into his chest and sighed. "This sucks Clay." Clay rubbed her back. "I know baby, it sucks big time."

Chapter 11

Clay and Shelby redressed without talking, each absorbed in their own thoughts. Clay was hoping Shelby was working her way back to him after his immense screw up the night before. The fact that she allowed him to love her physically, he was taking as a good sign. Shelby was fighting a losing battle emotionally. Clay had hurt her last night, yet she craved him. He brought her body to life in ways she never thought possible. It wasn't just the physical either. They were in tune with each other. He got her, really understood her. When she couldn't express her feelings he knew what she was going to say. Shelby gulped back a sob. She had to go back inside and she didn't want her Mom to know she was upset. Her Mom had been through so much.

They faced each other plucking off

errant pieces of straw and smoothing down tussled hair. Clay cupped Shelby's face and kissed her on her lips. She could still taste herself on him and she wondered if he could taste himself on her. They pulled apart each sighing in silent protest, and headed back inside. Half time was well over with and their parents and Clays aunt and uncle had the decency to not comment on their long absence. They took their place back on their chair and ottoman. Shelby sitting between Clays outstretched legs leaning back against his muscled chest both needing the contact. Clay put his head down to the side of her face and placed a discreet kiss on her cheek.

"More Shel's." He whispered to her. "I'm going to give you more."

Shelby leaned her cheek against his. She didn't answer him. She didn't want to start crying again.

The day ended with Clays aunt and uncle saying goodnight. They had all stuffed themselves on finger foods and because they had stayed awake until midnight the night before they were all tired. Clay's dad and Grace had an appointment the next day at State with a Private Investigator that they were going to hire to dig into what was happening with Shelby's Mom. Shelby needed to get to the airport so it was decided the three of them would make the long drive. Clay would stay with Shelby while she waited to board and Jed and Grace would meet with the PI then return to pick Clay back up.

Shelby trudged up the stairs to pack and her Mom followed. Jed and Clay remained in the living room. Shelby and her Mom skirted any Clay questions for part of the time. Shelby knew her Mom was concerned about their new relationship so she finally gave her the opening she needed by telling her Mom she had a great time being with her and especially meeting Clay. Grace grasped the opportunity and asked what was going on between them. Shelby was honest with her answers. She told her Mom she really cared for him, but was concerned with the distance, that he made her feel special. Shelby didn't tell her about their disastrous evening at the Elks. She also told her Mom that she felt a wonderful connection with him, that she thought he could be special that they were so in tune with each other. When her Mom was satisfied that Shelby was okay they talked about other things including the upcoming engagement party that Grace was giving Sara and Danny at the end of next month. When Shelby had everything packed she left her suitcase on the bed, laid out her travel clothes and she and her Mom returned to the living room. Jed and Clay had been discussing something, which ended abruptly upon their return.

"Jed, you ready for bed?" Grace asked.

Jed smiled up at his beautiful woman and stood up. "Yes, darling I'm ready." They climbed the stairs giggling like teenagers as Clay and Shelby watched.

"They are cute together." Shelby said.

"My Dad loves her Shelby. Really, really, loves her."

"I'm pretty sure my Mom loves him too. It's so strange to see her with another man, yet when I see them together, it's seems so right."

"Yea, it does. I'm glad you're okay with them. It be hard if you weren't."

They sat together watching the final Bowl game of the day.

"Clay will you come out to Sara's engagement party with your dad? I know you're invited. Will you be able to get away?"

"I hope to. I want to see you. I'll have to set things up here and see what happens with the PBR. There's also a cattle sale near that time that I have to go to."

"I hope you can too."

"Shelby, how are we leaving us?"

Shelby knew what he was talking about. Were they dating? Could they date others?

"I'm not going to tell you not to date anyone Clay. If you want to you can."

"I guess that means you can too." Clay said solemnly.

"Here's the thing." Shelby took a deep breath. "If you want to be with someone else then what we have... Well maybe it was just a whirl - wind romance. If you, we, don't want to be with anyone else well then maybe, just maybe we have something special."

Clay nodded. He knew mere words were not what held relationships together. He prayed he had given Shelby what she needed so she wouldn't want to be with anyone else.

That night Clay and Shelby made love and talked throughout he night. Neither wanted to waste their last precious hours sleeping.

The ride to State for the first time ever was too short. Clay and Shelby sat in Clay's dad back cab seat holding hands and talking quietly. At the airport Shelby hugged Jed goodbye and thanked him for taking care of her Mom. She then hugged her Mom. Grace got weepy and Jed pulled her in to comfort her after they released each other. Clay took Shelby's wheelie luggage and they strolled in to the terminal. The airport wasn't a large hub so Shelby was able to wait with Clay in a small lounge after she had checked her bag, before going through security. Shelby luckily had brought her passport with her, as an alternative ID option for the airport so not having her license was not going to poise a problem. They sat next to each other trying to make conversation light.

A line began to form and they knew it was time for Shelby to go through security. Clay took her hand and led her over to a small alcove that allowed for a small amount of privacy so he could kiss her goodbye. They held on to each other like they were life rafts in a swirling sea. Clay was choking his tears back and Shelby's feel unchecked down her cheeks.

"I'm going to miss you so much Shel's."

Shelby nodded into his shirt. "Me too." She eked out.

Clay bent down and ravished her mouth with heated loving kiss. He pulled away leaving them both shaking. "I think I love you, baby."

Shelby looked at her handsome man. His eyes were wet and she knew deep down he was special. "I'm so close Clay. I'm so close it frightens me."

"I know baby. Don't be scared. Take a chance on me, Shelby."

Shelby pulled him down for a final kiss. She pulled away wiping her tears, reached for her small carry on and walked to security. Clay watched her go. He felt like a knife was gutting his insides. He reached up to wipe his hand over his face and realized his cheeks were wet. Shit! He was crying. He couldn't remember the last time he cried. He wiped his face with his palm and plastered a fake smile on his face as he watched Shelby go through security. When she got through to the other side, he waved to her and she waved back. She then placed her hand over her chest and gently patted her heart. Clay didn't know why, but he returned her gesture patting his heart, his breaking heart.

Chapter 12

The drive back to the 5 Star was quiet. Grace and Jed tried to make small talk with Clay but they soon gave up. Clay felt as if his insides were being torn out. How could one little woman bring him to knees in a just one short week? When they got back to the 5 Star Clay headed to the barn and saddled his horse. He grabbed some water and a leather roll of tools and headed out. He told his Dad he was going to check fence lines.

Grace and Jed stood on the front deck and watched him head out. "My boys hurting." Jed spoke quietly to Grace.

"Shelby' s going to be hurting too. I hope they'll be okay Jed."

Clay rode where the snow drifts

allowed and checked miles of fence line. He shored up one area that had buckled, but aside from the one spot he hadn't had to do much. The sun was getting ready to set and the temperature had taken a severe dip. He turned his horse towards home.

When he got home Eddie took his horse and Clay told him to give him an extra long rub down, some extra grain and also to put a blanket around him. Clay walked into the mudroom off the side of the kitchen, took off his outerwear and his spurred boots. He walked into the kitchen and found Grace baking while his dad relaxed on the couch watching TV.

"Son, you were gone for a long time. Fences okay?" Clay knew that was a double entandra. He was really asking if he was okay.

"Yea, Dad. I rode most of the North range and part of the East. Only had to fix one spot."

Grace went to the oven and pulled out a plate covered with foil. "Clay I saved you some dinner." Grace put the plate on the table, removed the foil and got him a napkin and silverware. Clay realized he was hungry so he thanked Grace and sat down to eat.

"Grace has Shelby checked in yet?" he asked.

"Not yet. She should have landed a couple hours ago. I am surprised she hasn't called yet." Then, Grace's head snapped up and she looked at Clay.

"Clay did you give Shelby your home number?"

"No." he said shaking his head. Clay put down his fork. "Didn't you?"

"No." Grace answered. "I'm so use to using cell phones I never thought about it."

Clay jumped from the table and grabbed the phone from the wall. "Grace what's her number?"

Grace recited her number to Clay and he punched in the corresponding buttons. "Clay." Jed said gently. "She might be sleeping, remember the time difference." Clay looked to Grace and she just shrugged her shoulders. The phone started to ring and after the fourth ring a sleepy Shelby mumbled a hello.

"Hi, it's me. You made it home?"

"Hi." He heard her yawn. "Yea, I didn't have your home phone number I emailed my Mom. I guess she hasn't seen it yet."

"I guess I woke you. I'm sorry." Clay took the hand held into the mudroom for privacy. "I just wanted to make sure you got home alright."

"Thank you. Are you okay? You sound, I don't know...quiet."

Clay chuckled. "I'm in the mudroom. I wanted some privacy." Shelby giggled.

"I got home no problem. I was so tired I went to bed after I emailed my Mom."

"I miss you already." Clay said in a hushed voice.

"I miss you too Clay."

"I know your tired baby, but we have to figure out how to stay in touch with each other keeping the time difference in mind and the fact that if we phone each other all the time we'll go broke." He heard Shelby laugh and pictured her lying in his bed that morning.

"Actually, I thought about this on the plane. I was hoping you wanted to stay in touch."

"Shelby, did you doubt it? Really?"

Shelby sighed audibly. "So here's a possible solution...Skype."

"Skype that computer thing that lets us see each other like video conferencing?"

"Exactly. I already have an account. If you set one up we can Skype each other at pre set times."

"That's great. I'd still get to see you."

"Okay well my Mom has my Skype account information on her iPad. Get it from her. You Skype me tomorrow at 6:00pm your time and it will be 9:00pm here and I'll be waiting for it. My Mom can help you. Set it up tonight okay? I even have it on my iPhone."

"Okay I'll get on it." Clay already felt a little better. "I'll talk to you tomorrow. I'm sorry I woke you, but I'm happy to hear your voice."

"You're sweet, Clay. Thank you. I'll talk to you tomorrow."

Ok. Shel's...Miss you."

"Miss you too, Clay."

When Clay got off the phone Grace gave him a little smile. "She got home okay?"

"Yea, she... Oh crap Grace I'm sorry did you want to talk to her?" Grace laughed. "That's okay Clay. I'm glad one of us talked to her."

"Grace, will you help me set up a Skype account?"

"Sure, honey. Is that how you're going to stay in touch? It's a good idea."

Grace got out her laptop, while Clay went to get his. Clay helped her tap into their wireless network. Once she was online and Clay was online, Grace helped him create an account and showed him how to make calls and receive them. They Skyped each other for practice. It was a pretty cool application and he loved that he'd be able to see Shelby. Grace also gave Clay Shelby's email address and he also asked for her home address.

Clay thanked Grace for helping him and also thanked her for dinner. Her keeping a meal warm for him was a real 'Mom' thing to do and he appreciated her gesture. Clay took his laptop up to his room. After he showered Clay got back online and sent Shelby flowers that she'd receive tomorrow. He sent her a dozen white roses. He typed in the message area that would be included with the flowers, 'More.'

Clay shut his computer and climbed into his bed. The sheets still smelled of her. He was going to have a hard time washing them. He didn't want to wash her scent from them. Clay drifted off to sleep.

Shelby woke up the next morning feeling bereft. She missed sleeping with Clay, when they slept, anyway. Shelby did her laundry and cleaned her little apartment. She organized her lessons for her classes and worked out at the Y. After food shopping

she sat down to watch some TV and the
doorbell rang. A delivery person held a long
white box with a large blue bow accenting it.
Shelby tipped the young boy and brought the
box in to her kitchen She slipped the bow
from the box and opened the top of the box
to find gorgeous white long stemmed roses.
The card that lay on the flowers simple said,
'More.' Clay, how sweet she thought. She
put the roses in a vase and propped the card
up next to them.

It was 9:00pm and Shelby sat on her
bed, leaning against her head board with her
laptop propped open at her side as she
watched TV. The little ding sounded
signaling someone was trying to Skype her.
Shelby quickly answered and Clay appeared
before her on the screen.

"Hi Baby." He smiled brightly at her.
"What the hell are you wearing?"

"Clay, hi." She laughed when she
realized he could see her p.j.'s. "It's an old

friends football jersey. I always wear it. It's soft."

"Shit, I'm jealous of a football jersey." Shelby laughed and snuggled in for her Skype conversation with her sexy guy.

They told each other what they had been doing. Clay told her he had spent a lot of time working the ranch. His dad had actually put in some time too, and that had freed him up to go to Briggsby to run some errands. He also told her that Ricochet his prize bull was getting some good press and he hoped that would help with the PBR committee. She told him what she'd done throughout the day. She asked about her Mom and Clay told her she was good. He told Shelby how she had saved dinner for him the night before. Shelby could tell that meant a lot to him. Clay told Shelby he was meeting Ricky for a couple beers after dinner. Shelby told him to have fun, that she was just going to bed. They closed out of Skype reluctantly. Before getting off Shelby tapped her chest over her heart and Clay returned the gesture. Shelby smiled that he did it and blew him a kiss, before signing off.

It niggled at Shelby that Clay's night was just starting and that he was going out. It shouldn't have. She knew Clay cared for her. Yet their New Years Eve date had muddied the waters. Shelby would never know if he fooled around anyway, well unless Liz, Lars or Mac witnessed it. Shelby laughed. If Liz saw him with another girl she'd call her immediately. If Lars saw him with someone, he'd tell Liz and Mac, and if Mac saw him with someone, he'd tell Lars, who would tell and Liz, and Mac might even call her himself. After all he had been interested in her. Shelby knew if she hadn't liked Clay so much she would definitely gone for Mac.

Shelby opened her laptop again and sent off an email to Liz just to keep the friendship alive. She didn't ask Liz to keep an eye on Clay. She didn't even say much about him except that they had made up. For the second time that night Shelby closed her laptop.

Chapter 13

Days turned into weeks. Shelby fell back into her normal routine; morning gym workouts, teaching all day, grading papers at night, sometimes dinner with girl friends. She did venture out to the bars and clubs on weekends, but she had no desire to hook up with the men that expressed interest in her. She and Clay kept in touch via email and Skype but the time difference and their busy schedules prevented them from communicating daily. Clay told her he was going to be at the engagement party. The cattle sale he was going to was Thursday and Friday so he was cleared to go. He and his dad were flying out Saturday together and would take a taxi to the party when they landed, since the party would already be underway.

Shelby's Mom flew in a few days

before the party and they spent time looking for wedding dresses, seeing Sara's wedding gown and doing tons of pre wedding things. Grace also had spent time making sure the engagement party was on track. Her Mom seemed different Shelby couldn't put her finger on it. Grace stayed in a hotel room since Jed would be flying in and joining her. Shelby had told Clay he could stay with her.

The night of the party arrived. Her Mom was in full hostess mode, as was she. They worked the room, made sure everyone was happy, talking, and enjoying the food and drinks. They were using a DJ who was playing a variety of music for young and old alike. Shelby noticed her Mom watching the door. She knew she was waiting for Jed. Shelby found herself watching it as well. She couldn't wait to see Clay. She hoped their spark was still there, she wasn't sure. They spoke as much as they could but the distance had taken the wind out of the sails so to speak.

Tonight Shelby had dressed in a blue shimmery spaghetti strapped dress. She couldn't wear a bra with it because there was no back to the dress. The edge of the dress ran down her sides until it got to just above her ass. Then the material met up again and fell in a swishy cut mid thigh. Shelby knew she looked good in it. The dress also looked great coupled with her 'fuck me' shoes that she had worn on New Years Eve, which was a plus because she wanted to wear them for Clay. Shelby's nipples protruded through the thin material and she wore a very, very small black thong.

Shelby was out on the dance floor with her Mom and Sara. A slow song started playing and Danny claimed Sara. Grace and Shelby were walking off the floor when her Mom was grabbed from behind and pulled backwards into a chest of a friend of her fathers.

"Ray let me go." Grace said as she swatted at him, not wanting to make a scene.

Shelby watched as the scene unfolded before her eyes. Ray had his arms firmly around her Mom and her Mom was not happy about it. Before Shelby could intervene a deep voice barely containing it's fury spoke from behind them.

"Take your hands off my wife."

Ray turned with Grace still in his arms.

Jed loomed over them. Grace wriggled out of Ray's arms and leapt into Jed's arms. Jed pulled her close to him with one arm.

"Your husband!" Ray yelled.

By now most of the partiers were watching the scene unfold.

"Yes, my husband." Grace reached up and pulled Jed down for a quick kiss. The kiss seemed to ground Jed and she felt the tension leave his body.

"Hi wife, I missed you."

"I missed you too."

"You're married?" One of Graces best friends asked.

"Yes, this is Jed. Jed Jones, and we were married on Tuesday."

Shelby watched Clay standing next to his dad. He was as surprised as she was at their parent's announcement.

Shelby, Clay, Sara, and Danny along with her Mom's friends eagerly crowded around the newlyweds dispensing congratulatory hugs. Finally, after many heartfelt enthusiastic well wishes from friends, the four kids finally got the two of them alone.

"Didn't you want us there?" Shelby asked.

Jed answered. "We did. It was the one thing missing, but it was spur of the moment. I didn't want to wait any longer. Don't be mad at your Mom."

"Mom, we aren't mad, we love that you're happy." Shelby answered.

"Why didn't you tell us?" Sara asked.

Jed held his hands in an 'I surrender' motion.

"Jed wanted to. He wanted to call you all on Tuesday. I wouldn't let him."

"Mom why?" Sara insisted.

Grace looked at Sara, "I wanted this to be your day honey, yours and Danny's. We were going to tell you tomorrow at breakfast."

Shelby laughed, "How Mom of you." She teased. Clay still hadn't said anything. He was standing next to Shelby. She noticed his eyes were on her, not their parents but on her.

Her Mom's friends over ran their family meeting with more congratulatory hugs and Clay used the distraction to take Shelby by the elbow and lead her to the side of the room.

"What the hell are you wearing?" He was almost growling.

"Clay, I thought you'd like it." Shelby asked surprised by his attitude.

"Cripes, I do, shit Shelby, I do, but so does every other male in this room." Clay looked her over again and recognized the shoes she had on. He looked back up to Shelby with a smile that almost brought Shelby to her knees. Even though they saw each via Skype she had almost forgotten how devastatingly handsome Clay was. His body language became tight and guarded and he shifted restlessly. He leaned in to Shelby and whispered huskily in her ear. "Woman I am so hard right now I could cut diamonds." Shelby shivered at his lustful tone.

Shelby reached up for Clay and curled her little hand around his neck. She pulled him down till their mouths met. Clay groaned into her and Shelby shivered at the contact. The spark was still there. It was more than a spark it was a wild fire. Their bodies melted together and Shelby had to resist the urge to grind against him. He was addicting. They separated from each other at the same time, remembering where they were.

Clay placed his hands at her waist keeping them physically connected. "Shel's I have missed you so much." Shelby put her hands on Clays biceps. She could feel the muscles beneath his suit jacket. Shelby gazed appreciatively into his handsome face. "I've missed you too."

Her heart pitter - pattered. He was without a doubt, hot. He was wearing a dark suit paired with his dress up black cowboy boots. He had on a bolero tie that boasted a blue-green stone embellished with silver. The stone made his green eyes sparkle. A big silver belt buckle rested below his narrow waist. He was dripping testosterone. Shelby felt her self grow damp just looking at him.

"I want to hold you, baby, and kiss you.

It's been too long. Is there any place private we can go?'

"Clay, I can't just drop out of sight. It's my sister's engagement party. All our friends are here."

Clay groaned in frustration. "Shelby that dress, shit, I don't know if I can watch you flit around all night in that dress, and those shoes."

Shelby pulled him in for a warm embrace.

"Clay, you say the nicest things." She rested her chin on his chest and tilted her head up so she could look at him.

"I'm serious!" he groaned.

"We'll have alone time in a few hours. Right now I want to introduce you to some friends of mine and I want to talk to my Mom some more. You didn't know did you?"

"About them getting married? No. I knew they had worked out whatever trouble that was going on with your Mom. My dad told me about it on the plane ride here."

"My Mom told me that too. I'm glad she's safe now. I thought she was smiling so much because of that. Ha, she was smiling because she married your dad!"

"Is it weird that we, you are dating and they're married? We're like step siblings now, right?" Clay looked at Shelby with such a frustrated little boy face that she burst out laughing.

"Yes, you are now, officially my step brother." Shelby reached up and tucked a stray lock off his forehead. "Are you too weirded out by this? We can just be friends?" Shelby asked him seriously. Clay took her hands in his.

"Shelby, You know how I feel. Nothings changed, has it?"

"Nothings changed with me. How about you?"

"Are you asking me if I've dated anyone since you've left the answer is no."

Clay bracketed her face with his hands as he looked down on her so tenderly Shelby's heart squeezed.

"Shel's have you dated anyone?"

Shelby saw his jaw tense and his lips thin. His eyes darkened and she thought he might even be holding his breath.

Shelby put her hands on his hands that held her face.

"No, I have not dated."

Clay visibly sighed in relief. He flashed her the most brilliant smile.

"So, you're still my girl?"

"Yup, especially now."

"Why especially now?"

"Now, my handsome cowboy, because you are here, with me."

Shelby turned her head into his hand and kissed the inside of his palm.

Clay leaned down and gave her the softest open - mouthed kiss Shelby had ever had. It was sweet, but seductive. Shelby moaned her arousal and held him tightly. Her nipples were so hard they ached. Clay lifted from the kiss and stroked her cheek with his thumb.

"I know you want to stay here baby." He said huskily. "But if you continue to kiss me like that we aren't going to."

Shelby leaned her forehead against his chest clutching his lapels.

"Clay?'

"Ummm?"

"You look great in this suit." Shelby told him quietly.

Clay chuckled. "Thanks baby. I already told you what I think of that damn dress."

Now Shelby laughed. She took his hand in

hers and they rejoined the party.

As usual Clay got his share of seductive glances. Just like in Wyoming the woman touched him flirtatiously, when they could and the men gave him berth until they got to know him. Shelby and Clay remained connected the entire night in some fashion, holding hands, touching thighs, Clay's arm around her waist or shoulder. Clay couldn't keep his hands off her, and Shelby didn't mind at all. He noticed she seemed to like his possessive overtures. He was happy about that since they weren't going away.

They spent some time with their parents. Jed related the story of how they married. Shelby watched her Mom looking up at Jed. Jed never took his hands off her. God, Shelby thought they are so in love. She was happy for her Mom. Clay seemed to be happy too. Grace told them she and Jed were taking them and Sara and Danny, out to brunch the next morning. They all had so much to talk about.

The party wound down. Clay wanted to push the stragglers out the door and Shelby laughed at his impatience. When the final person left Shelby and Clay helped Sara and Danny carry their gifts and cards to the car. Grace settled the final tab splitting the bill with Danny's parents. Sara and Danny left and Clay and Shelby walked inside.

"Dad, Grace." Clay started speaking solemnly. Shelby bit her lip wonder what he was up to. "I need you to handle this as mature adults, but I'm staying at Shelby's tonight." Grace looked up from rummaging through her purse and Jed had to let what Clay said sink in, before he laughed so loud a waiter clearing a table looked up.

"Touché son." Jed clapped Clay on the back.

Shelby drove her and Clay to her little apartment. He had already seen what her apartment looked like because during one of their Skype sessions Shelby had walked her laptop around the apartment so he could see where she lived. She unlocked the door and they entered. Clay dropped his over night bag next to the door, turned back and shut the door clicking the cheap lock into place. He turned back to Shelby who had shrugged out of her coat. He bent his knees and reached his hands around her to cup her ass pulling her up to straddle him. He was already hard. Their mouths collided in a frenzy of lips, tongue and moans.

Clays hands were firmly on Shelby's bare ass as he turned and placed her back against the door they just entered. When he had her balanced against the door he took one hand off her and cupped her breasts through the thin dress. Shelby was grinding against his ridged cock. The friction of his hard cock, under his pants, rubbing her clit through her satin panties was sending delicious ripples through her saturated folds. Clay shifted Shelby so she was perched and straddling one of his slightly bent thighs. He needed both of his hands free. He balanced her against the door and used both hands to reach under the hem of her dress and lifted it over her head. Her breasts jutted out to him, her nipples dark and extended were begging for attention. He dipped his head to pull one into his mouth to suck and swirl it with his tongue. Shelby groaned. She was moving unabashedly rubbing herself against his muscled thigh. Shelby could feel his pants were wet with her arousal.

Shelby used her hands to push his jacket off and lower his bolero. She was probably choking him. She needed his shirt off, now. Clay helped her loosen and lift his bolero over his head. Once it was off him Shelby grasped the spaces between some of his shirt buttons and yanked it apart. Clay stopped his sucking on her tit to look at what his woman had done. She looked at him with an almost feral look in her eyes and he gave her a little quirky smile. Shelby was breathing hard and she went to rip the rest of his shirt buttons apart but Clay beat her to it grasping his shirt and pulling it apart. His powerful chest bulged as he discarded the now ruined shirt. He quickly pulled it from his arms and threw it over his shoulder.

"Clay your pants. Off, get them off." Shelby panted.

Clay removed his thigh from between her legs and let her find the floor with her 'fuck me' heels. He unfastened his belt, unbuttoned and unzipped his slacks removing them and his boxers in record time. Shelby was pulling her clothes off at the same time.

They stood staring at each other naked and glistening from their efforts. "Shelby you are so fucking beautiful." Clay said before he grabbed her ass and forced her to straddle him. Again he pushed her back against her door. Clays hips pinned her against the door as their hands rubbed and caressed each other intimately. Clay lifted Shelby slightly to poise her over his throbbing cock. He lowered her slowly, her gushing tight sheath greedily welcoming him home. Shelby wrapped her legs and 'fuck me' heels around Clays hips and rotated her hips in tight circles as Clay thrust into her like a piston on a train. Shelby greeted each thrust with a tightening of her cores Kegel muscles. She was literally sucking him off from her insides.

Shelby had never been so turned on. She leaned in to suck on Clays neck and bit him gently. Clay's balls tightened and Shelby's womb quaked. They exploded together. Clay clenched his ass and bucked into her uncontrollably. Shelby screamed his name raking her nails along his wide shoulders. Her clit was vibrating and her walls spasm intensely as warm liquid rained out of her core coating Clays cock, balls and her quivering pussy. Clay held Shelby tight as she panted into his chest. He remained inside her and he walked them to her bedroom. He fell back on the bed cushioning Shelby as she fell on top of him.

"Clay, I'm so wet. I made you wet. What the heck was that?"

"Baby I think you ejaculated."

"Oh God that was hot I came so hard. Thank you."

"You never need to thank me for loving you the way you should be loved. I just wish I could do it every day."

Shelby snuggled into his chest as he rubbed her back.

"I miss you, Clay. I miss you every night when I get into bed. I miss talking with you, face to face. I miss seeing you, listening to you, dancing with you. I miss us."

Clay let her sweet words wash over him. He played his hands lightly over her lower back, hips and rear.

"I miss you too baby. When you left, I felt so

empty. We have something Shelby. Something I want to explore, but I don't know how to clear across the country."

Shelby nodded into his chest and kissed him over his heart.

"Shel's, when you pat your hand over your heart what is that?"

Shelby hesitated before talking. My Mom taught us that. When we were swimming competitively in the big arenas or playing games she would do that little pat over her heart to tell us she loved us.

Clay didn't speak. His arms tightened around her little frame. "Could you love me Shel's?"

Shelby cautiously sat up straddling him. Clay was still inside her and she didn't want to jostle him out. She liked the bond. She rested her palms on his chest and found his beautiful green eyes with hers.

"I love you Clay. I tried not to. You hurt me

on New Years Eve. I'm so afraid of loving you and getting hurt."

Clay reached up to her face with one of his hands and cupped her chin.

"Baby I'm so sorry for that. You have no idea how often I've replayed that night in my head."

"Do you love me Clay?"

"With every fiber in my body, Shel's. I have no desire to be with anyone else. I think of you all the time. I wonder what your doing, how's your days going. I hate the weekends the most. I hate that you're out at the bars and some guy may try to make a move on you and I'm not there. It's not that I think you'd do anything. I just don't even want another guy near you. It makes me crazy. I miss sleeping with you in my arms. But you know what, I miss talking with you more than anything. Don't get me wrong, I love having sex with you, but I miss talking with you. When I'm with you everything just makes sense. Shelby, I love you so much. I won't hurt you baby. I won't I promise."

Shelby felt Clay come to life inside her. She rotated her hips to encourage his ardor. Clay groaned and flexed his hips to drive himself deeper inside of her. She felt him expand within her walls and moaned her approval. Shelby moved her hips on Clay and set a slow sensuous pace. They touched each other reverently their moans a symphony of their passion. Shelby reached behind her to massage Clays tightening sacks. Clay wanted Shelby to orgasm with him so he reached between her legs and strummed her clit. They were so in tune with each other's body that they knew just where to touch, just where to stroke, how to caress, massage and kiss each other to drive the other wild. They erupted simultaneously. Shelby's pelvis jerked uncontrollable as her walls squeezed Clays cock tightly. Clay dug his heels into the mattress as he bucked rapidly shooting his warm semen into her gripping channel. Shelby collapsed on top of Clay's chest sated and exhausted. Neither of them spoke, neither of them could.

Shelby slid off to cuddle Clays side, his now soft cock plopping out of Shelby's wet sheath. Clay tucked her into his body and then affectionately kissed the top of her head. Shelby reached down and pulled her top sheet up to cover them. She nestled her cheek where Clays shoulder met his chest and splayed her hand over his sculpted chest. Clay rested his one hand on Shelby's hip and with his other hand he covered her hand that was on his chest. They were asleep within a minute.

Chapter 14

Clay and Shelby awoke to the suns rays bouncing on their faces. They hadn't moved from the position they had fallen asleep in, the night before. Shelby stirred and Clay stroked her hip letting her know he too was awake.

"I haven't slept that soundly in a long time," remarked Shelby.

"Me neither." Clay said as he stretched his other hand over his head and yawned.

"Mr. Jones I think you tired me out."

"Ms. Jensen I wish I could tire you out every night." Clay kissed her lightly on her forehead. "But right now I need to use your bathroom."

Shelby moved so Clay could get up. Shelby missed his warmth as soon as he left her bed. She rolled on to her back and stared up at the ceiling. Clay was a masterful lover. He always took care of her needs, always made sure she experienced pleasure. Last night she'd come with such force she'd drenched them both. Shelby shivered at the memory and her nipples pebbled. Clay returned to the bed and before he could pull Shelby back into his arms she jumped up to use the bathroom.

Back in bed they lay entwined. Their hands played gently over the others bare skin, craving the others touch. "What time is brunch?" Clay asked. "Noon." Shelby responded. "Then I have to take you back to the airport."

"I need more time with you, Shel's." Clay murmured into her hair.

"When you leave I think it may hurt even more than the last time. When do you think we can see each other again?"

"I don't know. I've wanted to tell you

something though." Shelby stiffened that he was going to deliver bad news. Clay felt her body tighten.

"No baby it's good. I think it's great. I hope you do too."

"What?"

"We've been selected, The 5 Star, as a PBR stock bull contractor. My bulls are going pro." Shelby saw the pride in Clays face. His eyes sparkled just talking about it.

"Clay I'm so proud of you. This is great news."

"I'm pretty excited. I will be able to go to the events because dad won't have started football yet. No ranch from our county has ever qualified before." Clay spoke the sentence with more reserve. "This year we'll have two."

"Another ranch from your county was selected? Wow! Who's?"

"The Meed's."

Shelby felt like she'd been sucker punched. "Dana's ranch?" Clay watched Shelby for a reaction. If she was having one she was masking it well.

"Who's going with their bulls?" Shelby knew the answer before Clay even said it.

"Dana." Clay said quietly.

Shelby gripped the sheets and tried to maintain a calm exterior. Inside she was sick.

"Oh." Was all she could come up with to say.

"Shel's? I'm with you. I love you. I'm not going to throw this away."

Clay tipped her face up so he could watch her. So he could gauge what was going on in her mind.

"I know. It's just... You'll be spending a lot of time with her I imagine. She isn't going to fall out of love with you, Clay. All that time together, alone, to work her way back to you."

"She's been a friend of mine for a long time. I've only seen her a couple times since New Years."

"She moved back from New York? I didn't know that."

"Yea, her and Dave have been putting in extra hours on the ranch with their bulls."

Shelby didn't want to ask how he knew this. Her stomach was in knots. Why did she feel he was slipping away again? Clay felt Shelby withdraw from him and he sighed in frustration.

"Shelby, we've had such a great night. Please don't pull away. I love you. I'll see her, you know that, but I won't be with her in any other capacity than a bull contractor or friend. I promise. I pinky swear." Shelby smiled at his attempt to lighten the mood.

Clay bent his head and pressed his mouth to Shelby's. He licked along her lips and she finally invited him in. They kissed and held each other and talked, squirting the Dana issue, until it was time to shower for brunch. Clay felt the heavy cloud hanging over them. He knew it was better that he told her upfront about Dana, rather than her finding some other way. Then she'd think he had deliberately kept it from her.

Brunch was a fun affair. They celebrated their parent's nuptials and Clay told the rest of the family about the bulls going pro. Jed had already known and was acting the proud papa. Grace knew this was a big deal and told him she would send him baked goods when he traveled. Shelby was proud of Clay. She just couldn't shake the ominous feeling knocking on their door.

After brunch Shelby piled her Mom, Jed and Clay into her suv and drove them to the airport. She drove them to the departing flights curb and they all got out to get their bags from the car and hug goodbye. Jed and her Mom hugged her first and then walked away to give her and Clay some privacy. Clay was holding Shelby to him but with just enough space between so they could look at each other.

"Baby, I don't know what's going on in that beautiful head of yours and it's scaring me."

"I'm scared Clay. I'm scared of losing this, us. If the roles were reversed and I was going off on weekend trips with Mac, I think you'd feel the same way."

Clay's first thought was that Shelby was still thinking about Mac and that was not good. His second thought was that she was 100% correct. He would not be handling it as well as she was.

"You're right. If you were going away with Mac, I'd be crazy jealous." Clays honesty surprised her. "I'll send you where the events will be. Maybe you can fly in for some of them."

"Clay it's lacrosse season. I'll be working every day, except Sunday's, which I need to use to stay on top of schoolwork, laundry and other things. It was a nice gesture, but I don't see it happening."

"After lacrosse season. Would you come after lacrosse season? I'll buy your ticket."

Shelby hugged him tightly. "We'll see, okay."

Clay bent down and kissed her possessively, the hell with PDA.

"I love you Shelby. I'm already missing you."

Shelby kissed him back passionately. "I miss you already, too." It was not lost on Clay that she never returned his proclamation of love. Clay's chest tightened. He did not want to lose this woman. They finally separated and as Clay walked away he turned back one last time and patted his hand over his heart. Shelby returned the gesture. Grace was watching from inside the terminal, they were in love, she knew it. Oh please don't let either of them get hurt she prayed silently.

Chapter 15

When Shelby returned to her apartment there a newspaper page lying open on her kitchen table. It was opened to the classifieds section, Job Openings. One Ad was circled. It was a job opening in the Briggsby Regional District, high school English teacher. Shelby smiled. Clay wanted her to move to Wyoming. Her heart pitty - pattered inside her chest.

The weeks continued to fly by. Clay and Shelby resumed their efforts to stay close via Skype and emails. They would send each other funny cards once in the mail. Clay had sent Shelby more flowers when he had arrived home. Shelby had begun coaching lacrosse so their time was even more limited. The PBR circuit had started up and Clay was preparing his bulls for their first rodeo.

During the first weekend that Clay was at a rodeo Shelby received a call from an unknown number on her iPhone. She answered it and to her delight Clays voice greeted her.

"Hello?"

"Hey."

"Clay?"

"Yup, I got a cell phone. The cities I'll be in have service. We'll be able to keep in touch better."

"That's great. I'll save your number. How's it going?"

"It's pretty cool. Everything is top of the line. The bulls are housed in individual pens near the arena. No one is allowed near anyone else's bull except the owner. I provide all their care."

"Are you in a hotel nearby?"

"Yea, we all stay in the same place.

Sometimes the cowboys stay in their own trailers. There are a couple of long time contractors that have their own trailers too. Everyone hangs out after the rodeo. We have a few beers, grab pizza or burgers and then do it all over again the next day."

"Clay... Ummm.... Any buckle bunnies trying to sweep you off your feet?"

Clay laughed out loud. "Where did you learn that rodeo lingo?"

"I've been reading up on it."

"No baby they go for the cowboys not the bull contractors." Clay laughed again.

They talked for a little while longer and Clay told her he'd call her again later that night.

Clay was able to talk to Shelby more often now that he had a cell phone. He transported his bulls from event to event. The daily grind was tiring, but exhilarating. Clay had worked so hard for this opportunity. He wasn't going to waste it by getting lazy now. At night Clay noticed Dana always managed to end up at his table. She hadn't brought up the New Years Eve debacle and neither did he. It was nearing 11:00pm and Clay was just about ready to call it a night. It was getting rowdier than usual. A couple of cowboys and contractors were pretty drunk. Clays cell phone vibrated alerting him to an incoming call. He saw that it was Shelby so he moved to a quieter area of the bar to answer.

"Hey babe. Everything alright?"

"Yea, I was just thinking about you." Shelby said on the other end.

"I'm always thinking about you." Clay answered without hesitation.

Just then Clay was jostled from behind and two arms encircled his waist.

"Clay honey come on back to the table." Dana slurred loudly into the ear he had the cell phone pressed against.

"Dana..." Clays voice became muffled like he was covering the phone.

Shelby's insides lurched. Clay came back on the phone.

"I'm sorry baby. Dana's a little drunk."

"Yea, I heard."

"Listen Shel's I have to take her back to her room. I'm sorry I'd really like to talk to you more but she's toast. Can we talk later on?"

"Oh well actually, I'm on my way out." She wasn't.

Shelby heard Clay say. "Sit down in the chair before you fall down, shit!"

"Okay baby, I'll call you tomorrow." Clay said as clicked off.

Shelby tried to reason with herself. They were friends. He's looking out for her. He loves me. No matter what she said to herself she couldn't shake the jealous feelings that haunted her. Clay did call her the next day and the next, Shelby didn't answer. On the third day Shelby finally picked up the phone.

"Hello?"

"Where have you been? I've been calling you."

"I've been busy."

"Shelby don't be this way. I know you're upset about Dana, but I swear, nothings going on, we're friends."

"I know Clay, you've told me." Shelby's voice was cold, distant.

"What can I do baby to convince you. I'm not fooling around."

Shelby sighed loudly.

"I don't think you are Clay. It's just... I'm having a hard time with it, with her being there. With you taking care of her."

"Shit, Shelby. I don't want you upset. But I need to be here."

"I know you do, but why does she need to be there?"

"What do you mean?"

"Why is she there? Not her brother or Dad. Did you ever ask her why she was taking care of the bulls?"

"No...I... Never thought about it."

"Well I have. I've thought about it a lot. I even asked Liz about it. Liz said that she heard she was on the circuit because you were on the circuit. She loves you Clay. I know she's one of your good friends, but she wants more."

Clay was quiet as he processed what she'd said. "I haven't crossed the line with her Shelby." Clay said quietly. "I won't."

Shelby waited before responding. "I love you Clay. I miss you. I can't spend my nights worried she's going to find a way to wiggle into your heart."

"She won't. You need to trust me."

"I do trust you. I don't trust her."

"Okay Shelby I get it. I do, please don't not answer the phone again. I was worried. We have to keep talking. It's important especially when we are apart."

Shelby knew he was right. She never liked playing head games with guys and Clay wasn't just any guy.

"Okay, you're right, I'm sorry I didn't answer the phone, it's just my imagination was being active... Let's forget it okay? Tell what's been going on?" The conversation switched gears and they filled each other in on their activities. Clay knew Shelby was still worried, but there wasn't anything he could do to alleviate her fears. He needed to distance himself from Dana as much as possible.

Shelby's lacrosse season had come to a close. The school year was ending soon and Shelby smiled at her secret that she kept hidden from everyone except her Mom, who she knew had told Jed. She asked them not to tell Clay. Shelby had applied for the job in Briggsby and gotten it. She gave her notice at her school and slowly started to pack boxes to join her Mom and Clay in Wyoming. Her Mom told her she could live with them at The 5 Star or she could live in her house, the one her Great Uncle had left her Mom. Shelby said she'd stay at her Mom's place.

Clay and Shelby talked daily. He assured her was keeping his distance from Dana. Shelby told him she appreciated that he was taking her feelings into consideration. Although they spoke almost daily their conversations weren't as free flowing as before.

One afternoon while Shelby was packing

her doorbell rang. Pulling the door open she discovered Mac standing there. He grinned at her stunned reaction, he was unfairly gorgeous, and when she recovered she asked what he was doing there.

"I have business here. I called Liz and she gave me your address. I hope you don't mind?"

"No, I'm happy to see you. Come on in."

Mac looked at her apartment filled with boxes and settled a questioning look at her.

"Where you going?"

"Wyoming."

"No kidding? Really? That's great!"

"Please don't tell anyone, I'm surprising Clay."

"He still in the picture?"

Shelby playfully cuffed his arm. "Yes." She laughed.

"I have a meeting at 2:00. Could we go to dinner afterwards? Just friends?"

Shelby thought about it for a second. She was just going to dinner. He knew she was still with Clay. She didn't see the harm, plus she could catch up on Landgrove gossip. She knew she would have to tell Clay she had had dinner with Mac. She justified her impromptu dinner date by telling herself that Mac knew they were just friends and he wouldn't be putting any unwanted moves on her.

"Sure." She told him.

"I'll come back for you around 7:00pm."

"Sounds like a plan."

Around 6:00pm Shelby realized she was out of shampoo. She had to shower before dinner so she left her apartment to walk down the street to the nearby pharmacy. Shelby noticed two men getting into a van as she approached them, but her thoughts were elsewhere plus she lived in a nice neighborhood so she didn't pay them much mind. Shelby bought her shampoo and quickly jogged back to her apartment to get ready.

When she arrived back at her apartment she fit her key into the lock but didn't have to turn it since the door slowly opened on it's own. Shelby always locked her door, but she thought perhaps in her excitement of her moving and her haste to get ready for dinner with Mac maybe she had forgotten to. She stepped inside and pushed in the little lock button in the center of the knob. She headed back to her bathroom. A man jumped out at her from her bedroom as she rounded the corner. Shelby was stunned, not expecting the attack. She fell backwards on her wood floor forcing her breath from her lungs. The smell is what she first noticed, the tobacco, weed, motor oil smell that she had smelled many months earlier. The large motorcycle club man that Clay had beaten up quickly took advantage of her prone position and pounced on top of her effectively restrain her as another man came to help him. As Shelby twisted trying to get free she saw that his partner was the smaller man from the bar. Shelby couldn't scream because she had no breath. She continued to struggle but they held her down easily.

"Remember us bitch?" The larger man sneered down into her face his spittle landed on her lips forcing Shelby to turn her head to the side as she gagged.

Her stomach lurched and she fought to not throw up. The large man pushed her arms behind her back and sat on her stomach successfully trapping her arms underneath her own body. He held his calloused, beefy hand over her mouth. She still hadn't taken a breath yet, and she felt herself get light headed. She knew she was going to pass out soon. The smaller man held her legs down and was talking to the larger man but she couldn't decipher what he was saying.

Shelby thrashed side to side, but she was totally at their mercy. She fought to free one of her hands that was pinned under her back and finally succeeded. The victory short lived as the man that was sitting on her chest grabbed it and slammed it brutally onto the floor. Shelby heard a sickening crack and the men laughed saying 'how that must have hurt.' The agonizing pain she felt assured her that he had broken her wrist. The pain intensified when he brutally tucked her limp hand underneath her again, readjusting his body to ensure she couldn't wiggle free again.

The men greedily ripped off her clothes and began touching her intimately. Shelby was sobbing uncontrollably still gasping for small pockets of air. She felt the man holding her feet take his hands from her legs as he trapped them now by sitting on them. He used his freed hands to plunge into her intimate folds, then painfully breech her dry core with his fingers. The other man squeezed her breasts roughly, Shelby bit out a cry of pain. The men were talking to each other but Shelby couldn't grasp what they were saying, she knew they were getting ready to rape her. She fazed out, her mind snapping with the trauma. She was having an out of body experience. They press their fingers inside her and crushed her breasts in their rough hands. The larger man was aggressively pinching and twisting her nipples and she knew it should hurt, but she was numb now. She was wondering if were they going to kill her too?

Shelby vaguely heard someone knocking at her door. The men looked at each other and in hushed voices planned their escape. Shelby was shaking violently. Her moans were stifled under the palm of one of her attackers. A strong punch to her face rendered her useless as she gratefully slipped into nothingness.

Mac heard movement inside the

apartment. He banged louder calling Shelby's name. He tried the door but found it locked. When he heard a crash coming from within the apartment he knew something was wrong. Mac launched himself at the flimsy door shattering the lock as the door swung inwards. One of the hinges had blown apart too and the door lay askew. Mac followed the moans and found a naked Shelby in a fetal position with blood pouring from her nose. Her body was a mass of red marks. Mac recognized finger pad marks covering her breasts and hips. He knelt next to her and was relieved to see she beginning to come to. He quickly called 9-1-1 from his cell and grabbed a quilt off her bed.

Shelby was shivering uncontrollably. Mac knew she was in shock. Her eyes were glazed and unfocused. He stroked her hair and her back trying to be as gentle as possible.

"Shelby, Shelby, honey I'm here. You're going to be alright baby, the ambulance is on its way."

Shelby focused for a nano second and the fear Mac saw in her face tore at his heart. She seemed to understand she was no longer in danger but she was definitely traumatized. She tried to clutch the blanket around her tighter and cried out in pain. Mac saw that her wrist was lying at an unnatural angle. He helped her by tucking the blanket around her as he continued to comfort her by stroking her back.

The ambulance and police arrived and the apartment turned into organized chaos. The police were peppering Mac with questions as the EMT's worked on Shelby. They quickly had her up and on a stretcher. As they lifted her onto the gurney a small plastic card fell off her body and onto the floor. Mac bent down and held it out so she could see it. It was her license, the one she had lost in Wyoming. Mac wanted to stay with her but the police were insistent he couldn't go with her; he could only follow the ambulance. Mac started to follow the stretcher out the door and one of the officers tried to detain him for more questions.

"Listen you ass hole. That's my friend on that stretcher if you want to talk to me further you meet me at the hospital. Other wise back off or I'll bury you in so many lawsuits you'll be retiring before you are back on the beat."

The stunned officer backed up and his older partner put a hand on him to keep him calm.

"Lawyer?" The older partner said to Mac.

"Lawyer." Then Mac strode from the apartment.

Shelby flickered back to reality in the ambulance. She began to softly cry and the EMT's reassured her she was safe. They whisked her to an examining room and a young doctor assessed her injuries and sent her off to get her wrist x-rayed, then set.

Shelby's whole body ached. Her face was swollen and she couldn't breath out of her nose. Her wrist throbbed. She let her tongue smooth over her teeth checking to see if she'd lost any.

A nurse was stationed in her room and every few minutes reassessed her vitals. When she wasn't doing that she stood next to Shelby and spoke to her softly. A woman came in wearing a crime scene jacket. She introduced herself as a detective with the crime scene unit and asked if it would it be okay if she collected samples from Shelby's body. Shelby realized that the real reason the nurse had been hovering nearby was to make sure Shelby hadn't unknowingly cleaned off any evidence. Shelby nodded glumly and the crime scene lady began her meticulous examination. Although she wasn't really tuned in to what the CSI detective was saying Shelby knew the woman was carefully explaining what she was doing, as she was doing it. When she finished she motioned the all clear for two men in jackets with badges who had been waiting in the hall to enter the room.

The detectives questioned Shelby as the nurse carefully cleaned her. Shelby appreciated the fact that she was being careful to not expose her private areas to the detectives. Shelby answered as best she could. Her mind was still reeling and the silver lining was that she knew she was lucky to be alive. She explained that the men that attacked her in her apartment were the same men that had accosted her in Wyoming back in December. She told them how her boyfriend had intervened and beaten them up. Shelby also told the detectives that she learned the men were part of a local motorcycle club. She didn't know their names but their motorcycle clubs insignia was a tornado driving a motorcycle. She also told them how she had lost her license in the ruckus that night and surmised that's how they had found her. The one detective nodded and told her they had found her license lying near where she had been found.

The detectives were satisfied and said they would stay in touch but she needed to be careful until the men were caught. One of the detectives said perhaps hurting her was pay back for her boyfriend beating them up and maybe they would disappear thinking they had settled the proverbial score. The two detectives left and Shelby settled her head back on the raised head of the bed. She grimaced at her throbbing wrist that was now encased in a cast, and propped on a pillow at her side. The weight of what had happened sunk in and she started crying again.

Shelby was just settling her emotions down when Sara burst through the door followed by Danny. She was hysterical and Shelby ended up calming her down instead of the other way around. Mac entered the room but stood near the door. He didn't want to intrude. Shelby told them what had happened leaving out much of the detail. She started to weep again and Mac went to her bedside and took her unhurt hand in his.

"The main thing is that you're going to be alright Shelby."

Shelby nodded at him and sniffed in her runny nose. He reached for a tissue from the box on the side table and gently held it under her nose telling her to blow. Shelby blew, and then smiled at him. He was a really good guy.

Shelby asked for a sip of water, which Sara handed to her with shaky hands. After a sip she told them she didn't remember how the attack ended. Mac told her what had happened when he arrived for their dinner date. He then told Shelby with a little smirk she needed a new door.

Shelby smiled at him and said thank you. The doctor came back into the room and asked everyone to leave so he could talk to Shelby alone. They all left and Shelby steeled herself for what he might say. They had done a rape kit on her because she couldn't remember if she'd been raped or not. She knew they had touched her and pushed their fingers inside her but after that she'd spaced out.

"Ms. Jensen you have a broken wrist, a broken rib, a fractured nose, but it wasn't displaced, and contusions and cuts, but you were not raped."

Shelby started crying into her one hand she was so relieved she wasn't raped.

"I'm going to recommend that you spend the night here, but you'll be free to leave first thing in the morning. You need to take Tylenol with codeine tonight and then Advil, like clock work when you leave. I'm going to be sending our resident psychiatrist to come see you tonight. It's standard procedure." The doctor gave her a pat on her leg and Shelby thanked him and he left.

Sara, Danny and Mac reentered the room. Sara was weeping again and Danny was comforting her. Mac strode to her bedside and retook her uninjured hand. He knew what the doctor visit was about. "Shelby what did he say?" Mac asked quietly.

Sara looked up from blubbering on Danny's chest and looked positively frightened by what Shelby might say.

"Sara I'm fine. Really." Shelby was shakily assuring her. "I'll heal."

Mac looked at Shelby knowing she was omitting something. "Shelby." He whispered softly to her as he bent his head close to her. Shelby knew Mac would know what she'd left out. The word was so foreign to her, so ugly. She whispered to him. "I wasn't raped Mac."

Mac ran his hand gently through her hair. "Oh baby I'm so glad to hear that." Shelby could see his shoulders sag with relief.

Sara told Shelby she'd called their Mom and she was catching the first plane out. She'd be there in the morning. Shelby was transferred to a room upstairs. Sara,

Danny and Mac stayed with her until visiting hours were over. Sara kissed Shelby on the forehead and told Shelby she'd go to her apartment and pick up clothes for her for tomorrow. Danny placed a kiss on her forehead as well and told her he'd help Sara. Mac sat down in the chair next to Shelby's bed and made himself comfortable. Shelby's eyes were drooping she was so tired and the pain medication was kicking in. She dropped off to sleep.

When Shelby awoke a few hours later she saw that Mac was asleep in the chair next to her.

"Mac?"

Mac sat up rubbing his hands over his face and stretched his arms over his head.

"What are you still doing here? Didn't they kick everyone out?"

Mac smiled down at Shelby. "I told them I was your lawyer and that I was staying next to you until the men were caught."

"Oh Mac, that's so sweet, thank you. You must be exhausted. It's so late. You should go back to your hotel room and get some sleep."

"I'm actually catching the red eye in a few hours back home. I didn't want to leave you. I can sleep on the plane."

In the hallway Clay heard voices coming from Shelby's room. He stopped outside her doorway. He didn't want to barge in if the doctor was examining her. His dad had called him and told him that Shelby had been assaulted. He told Clay what he knew, which wasn't much. Sara hadn't been a wealth of information and it was hard to tell what she'd been saying with her crying the entire time. His Dad had driven Grace directly to the airport and she'd boarded the first flight east. She was flying into LaGuardia and taking a taxi to Shelby.

Clay heard Shelby's strained voice. He was a mess and needed to get control of himself. He didn't know how badly Shelby was hurt or even what had happened to her. He was sick with concern for her. After Clay had received the call from his Dad he had jumped into action. He finished taking care of the bulls, and then paid a small fortune to be privately flown into the closest airport, which was Morristown. Clay had to be back in North Carolina, at the arena before the rodeo started. Bull contractors were not permitted to leave their bulls for an extended period of time. Clay had gone to the head of PBR and explained what happened. He told them he just wanted to make sure his girlfriend was all right, that it was an emergency, but he'd be back to ready which ever one of his bulls got the draw that night. They were satisfied with his emergency excuse and how he had left a contingency plan so Clay had been cleared to go without penalty.

Clay listened to the other voice in the

room. He knew that voice. He moved closer to the door. His gut seized.

"Mac, thank you for saving me. If you hadn't come when you did... Well."

"You don't have to thank me sweetie. I'm glad you're going to be alright."

He heard Shelby say. "I guess we need to rain check our dinner date."

"Don't you worry we will be having that dinner. I'll be holding you to that." Mac replied playfully.

Clays heart shattered. He knew she'd been upset about Dana, but to go out with Mac. He was reeling. Clay didn't know whether to enter the room and beat the shit out of Mac, well try anyway, or walk away. She should have told him she was dating Mac. She had been so concerned about him and Dana and here she was going out on dates with Mac behind his back. He was a fool thinking he could make their relationship work. Clay backed away from the room and walked back down the hall from which he came.

"You know I'll have to bring Clay with me right?" Shelby teased Mac. Mac laughed good- naturally.

"Yea, I know. God I hope he knows how lucky he is."

"Thanks Mac, you're a true friend."

"You may not be so happy with me when you see your door."

Shelby laughed. Mac kissed her gently on the cheek.

"Take care little girl."

"I will and thank you for saving me." Mac left the room.

Clay flew down the stairs hoping to pound out the anger he was feeling. He needed to get out of there. He knew if he saw Mac that there would be serious blood letting and Clay couldn't risk being arrested. No one involved in any rodeo, from the stock contractors to the cowboys and cowgirls, were allowed to have an arrest record. Clay was seeing red and as the conversation he over heard replayed in his head he didn't know whom he was madder with, Mac for snaking him, Shelby for playing him or himself for falling for her lies.

Clay walked out the hospital doors and headed towards the parking garage. The place was somberly quiet since it was so late at night. The only reason he had even been allowed in was he had told the lady wearing the pink jacket behind the information desk that his wife had been brought in via an ambulance after an accident and he was just getting there now. Clay could hear the distant drones of cars on a nearby highway. He thought how different New Jersey was to

Wyoming. His Wyoming was peaceful, so serene. He loved where he lived. He had hoped to someday share that special peace with Shelby. He couldn't believe he had actually thought about forever with her, of having more. He was such a fool.

Clay headed towards his small white rental car digging into his pocket for the key as he approached it. Lost in self - reflection he never heard the steps that crept up behind him. His head was forcefully slammed into the top of the car doorframe. The wet warmth he felt on his face was blood. Clay tried to turn around but he was unsteady and struggling not to black out. As he stepped backwards hoping to confront his attacker he was zapped with electrical bolts that sent him painfully careening onto the pavement. His last coherent thought was that someone had used a Taser gun on him.

Chapter 15

Grace practically flew in to her daughter's room. Shelby was dozing lightly, her broken wrist still propped up on a pillow. A purple hue was forming on her skin that would culminate in two black eyes and there was an ugly large bruise already present on her cheek. Shelby woke up to her Mom stroking her forehead.

"Hey mom." She weakly whispered.

"Hey sweetie. I'm here." Her Mom's face was tight with worry and she looked tired.

Shelby started weeping and told her Mom what she could remember. She didn't leave anything out. The two detectives that had visited her the night before arrived at her door before Shelby had even had breakfast. She introduced them to her Mom and repeated what she had said the night before.

They thanked her and gave her one of their cards in case she remembered anything else.

"Mom, does Clay know?" Shelby asked when the detectives left.

"Yes sweetie, Jed called him. He was going to try to get here. I'm surprised he didn't. There is a technicality about leaving the bulls but Jed said he thought Clay could work it out."

"I need him Mom, I need to talk to him."

"I know honey. I'm sure he'll be here soon, be strong. Wait until you tell him about your new job and moving, he'll be so happy."

"Do you think it's the right thing Mom? Me moving?"

"I think you care for Clay very much and I know he cares for you. I normally wouldn't advise you to move for a man, but I'm there. It makes sense. You've always been a little country girl anyway. You've secured a job and now you'll be able to see if what you and

Clay have is the real deal."

"I want what you have with Jed." Shelby smiled knowingly at her Mom.

"I wish that for you too. Clays so much like Jed and you're so much like me. It's actually a little weird. You know?"

Shelby giggled, "I know."

Shelby was finally cleared to leave the hospital. She still hadn't heard from Clay. They drove to Shelby's apartment to gather some clothes and personal items. Grace had made a mandatory motherly decision that Shelby finally had agreed too. Since Shelby was moving to Wyoming anyway in the next week. Grace insisted she move the date up and fly back with her tomorrow, she had already bought her the ticket. Shelby found her phone still in her handbag and checked for messages. Much to her surprise there were none. Shelby moved to her bedroom for privacy and called Clay. She needed to hear his voice. Clay never picked up.

They arranged for Shelby's car and all of her belongings to be transported to Wyoming. Grace helped Shelby pack what was necessary and arranged for a cleaning service to come after the movers had left. Sara drove them to the airport and said a tearful goodbye. She was going to make sure the movers and cleaners did their job. Shelby tried to call Clay again before she boarded the plane and again he didn't pick up, she text him to call her, that she needed to talk to him.

Clay slowly came awake. So many things became apparent despite the fact that he was blind folded. One was that he knew he was in a moving vehicle. He fought to take in a deep breath that sent other informational tid bits racing to his sluggish mind. He was gagged with a rag that tasted of motor oil and although that alone was over powering, rotten fruit and dirt were smells he could also detect. His arms were secured behind him and his wrists were being held together with what felt like plastic ties. His ankles were tied together as well. His wrists were attached to his ankles forcing his ankles up towards his butt creating a very uncomfortable position for him. He was essentially hog-tied.

Clay tried to relax his breathing since the gag was making him nauseous and the sickly sweet smell inside the vehicle wasn't helping. He continued to pretend he was still unconscious hoping to garner more information. Two voices were talking somewhat near him.

"When you think he's gunna wake?"

"It won't be long. "Should I tase him again before he wakes up?"

"No, he ain't goin anywhere." The one voice chuckled. "We tied that cowboy up but good."

"He bled all over the floor, my sisters gunna be pissed."

"For Christ sakes Rip we can clean it up. Relax."

"Yea, I know just want to get him out of here and be done with this shit."

"It's all good man. We avenged ourselves tonight and in a few hours I'll be a 1% member."

"I know Meat. You gunna rock that patch!"

"I deserve it. Pansy ass Push should have backed us back in December."

"He's gunna be pissed when he finds out about the girl."

Clays breathing hitched when he heard that. He knew they were referring to Shelby.

"She's alive much better for her than

how I wanted to leave her."

"How much longer till we get there?"

"Two hours. Two hours and we kill this cowboy and I get my patch."

Clay tried to even out his breathing again. He knew what a 1% patch was and he had a sickening feeling that he was whom the guy was going to kill in order to get it.

Chapter 16

Shelby and Grace arrived safely in Wyoming and Jed welcomed her home and insisted she stay with them until she was able to use her wrist more efficiently. While Jed helped Shelby with her luggage she asked him about Clay. He told her he hadn't heard from him since the night of her accident. He also confided to her that he was concerned that Clay had not called her or him for that matter.

Shelby, her Mom and Jed were sitting around the large dining room table after dinner when the phone rang. Jed answered it and Shelby and Grace could see the anguish on Jed's face with whatever news he was receiving. Grace jumped up from the tale and placed her hand on Jed's back in a supportive gesture. Jed was pale and his lips had thinned into hard lines. Shelby knew what ever he was hearing was not good.

"Sheriff, Grace just returned from New Jersey with her daughter Shelby. Shelby was attacked two nights ago in New Jersey. The men that did it were two guys from the motorcycle club Road Twisters. Clay had an altercation with them back in December."

The sheriff said something and Jed thanked him and hung up.

When Jed hung up the phone he looked right at Shelby and she knew the news had to do with Clay. She began to shake and her chin quivered as she tried to hold back tears.

"Jed? What's happening?" Grace asked.

"That was the sheriff. He just got a call from the New Jersey State police."

Shelby was rocking in her chair and Jed's voice faltered and he had to look away.

"They just found Clay's rental car in the hospital parking lot. There's blood all over the door." Jed's voice cracked and he held his hand over his eyes trying to regain some composure.

"Oh God, Oh God, no, please no." Shelby was whispering her pleas into a fist that was covering her mouth.

Grace didn't know who to comfort they were both so distraught.

"We have to go to the sheriffs office."

"Why? Why do we have to go? Is he? Did they find? Oh God." Shelby was panicking and felt bile rise in her mouth. She ran to the bathroom and vomited. Her Mom followed her and held her hair back. There was nothing she could say to help her daughter or her husband.

Shelby returned from the bathroom. "Shelby they haven't found him. He's not… as far as they know he's alive. I don't know much more than that. Come on let's get to the sheriff's office."

As they drove towards town Shelby was sick with fear and Jed was visibly a wreck. "This is all my fault." Shelby whispered to Jed and her Mom.

"What? Why?" Jed asked.

"Because I left the bar that night at State. If I had just stayed and waited for Clay to explain things he would of never met those men. Oh God Jed I'm sorry. I'm so sorry."

"Shelby." Jed said in a tone that forced her to stop whimpering. "Those men are bad and yes circumstances had you and Clay running into them but don't you dare think this is your fault. Sweetie hold it together okay."

Grace placed her hand on Jed's arm and squeezed it. Jed was a good man and Grace knew he was dying inside yet he was emotionally strong enough to help her daughter who was crumbling with a few fatherly words.

At the sheriffs office they were brought in to a small conference room and quickly joined by the sheriff. The men shook hands and then the sheriff shook Grace's hand as well. Grace introduced him to Shelby. The sheriff ushered them all into chairs.

"Your information has really gotten the ball rolling Jed. No one should jump to any conclusion yet. Maybe that's not even his blood on the car."

"How'd they find the car?' Jed asked.

"It was in the hospital parking lot and someone noticed a cowboy hat laying near the door. The Good Samaritan picked the hat up to bring it to the hospitals front desk and that's when they noticed what they thought looked like blood on the car. They told the parking attendant who called the police."

Shelby squeezed her Mom's hand and leaned towards her. "Mom, Clay came. He came to the hospital." Shelby had so many different emotions clawing at her. She was distraught that Clay was missing yet she was relieved that he had come to check on her. She figured he was jumped before he even got inside.

The sheriff continued. "So I called the Wyoming DEA after I talked to you. They have a sizable interest in the activity of the motorcycle gangs out here. They have an agent that's been undercover for over a year now and she just happens to be imbedded with the Road Twister's. They have sent her an emergency call and are hoping to hear from her soon. She may be able to help us find these guys that we are assuming took Clay."

"We are assuming they took him right?' Asked Grace.

"Yea, our best guess is that they hurt Shelby here knowing Clay would come for her and then they grabbed him. It's only a guess but the timing and motive fit too well to be just a coincidence."

"Okay." Said Jed quietly. "What can I do?"

"Jed you know there is nothing you can do right now. Give us some time. We already have the DEA involved and the FBI is on stand by. If you want to go home…"

The sheriff never even finished his sentence before Jed interrupted him with a curt, "No! We'll be staying right here. You might need us." Jed's voice was cracking again. "You might need us." He said again this time so quietly that it scared Shelby.

"Okay Jed, I get it. You and your family stay here. I'll let you know the second I hear anything, alright?"

"Yea, thanks. I mean it Sheriff thanks." The two men rose from their chairs at the same time and Jed shook his hand again before the sheriff walked out the door.

Shelby, Jed and her Mon sat quietly waiting. Grace tried to keep her daughter and Jed calm but the anxiety they both were feeling cloaked the room and she finally gave up and started pacing right along with Jed. Shelby was sitting at the table with her forehead resting on her arms. Every few minutes she could be heard sniffing back her tears. Minutes turned into hours. Someone brought them coffee but all three cups remained untouched. Finally the sheriff flew in the door and quickly told them they had word and they were to follow him to his office.

The sheriff took a seat behind his desk that had a laptop on it. The sheriff turned the lap top screen around so it faced Shelby, Jed and Grace. On the screen was the face of a woman with short spiky dark hair, a nose ring and a leather neck cuff.

"Pixie this is Jed the boys father." The sheriff said by way of introduction. "Tell them what you just told me."

"Hey so here's what I know. Last December these two bone heads; Meat and Rip go against a command and head into State during a snowstorm. When they returned they had obviously gotten into a fight and they were pissed as all get out. They told everyone that some young cowboy had gotten the drop on them while they were messing with some whore in a bar." Shelby cringed knowing they were referring to her.

"Meat and Rip wanted the gang to go find the cowboy and beat the shit out of him. The head of the club told them to let it drop and told everyone to leave it be. You see the Road Twisters are trying to merge with the larger motorcycle club the Canyon Runners and the Canyon Runners don't want to take on a gang that gets in to trouble. They run too many illegal activities and they want to keep the cops as far away from them as possible. So any way I've gotten close to meat's old lady and when she drinks she talks. Seems that Meat and Rip have been planning to retaliate against your son for a while now. They didn't even know who he was but they had the girl friends license. So they have been AWOL for a week now and all hell has been breaking out trying to figure out where they are. Meat's old lady called Rip's sister and she told her that Rip has borrowed her work van. The sister sells fruit and shit at local farmer markets. Meat's old lady told me she thinks they went after the girl to draw the cowboy out."

The room was quiet and Jed spoke to Pixie. "Do we know where they are now?"

Pixie broke out into a huge smile. "Yes sir, we just got a warrant to track the van via it's satellite radio. My bosses have already called in the FBI now and they have traced the van, which is still moving to somewhere in Illinois on Route 80. The State Police have been notified. We are all keeping our fingers crossed."

"Pixie do you know where they are headed?" The Sheriff asked.

Pixie looked a little disturbed and Jed realized she was trying to hide something.

"What? Tell me."

"Sheriff maybe it's not something everyone should hear." She said quietly.

"Oh God." Shelby whispered.

"Look just tell us. We know the situations bad."

"Sheriff?" Pixie looked at him for guidance. The sheriff told her to go ahead.

"Okay so I told you about the possible merger. Well Meat wants to go into the merger with a 1% patch."

"Oh God." Jed croaked as he paled. Shelby knew what a 1% patch was and she started weeping again.

"Listen here's the thing about getting the patch. The kill has to be done in the presence of another 1% patched member. Meat has a brother who is a 1% member in Iowa. They aren't there yet. We think that's where they are headed. If he wants his patch and according to his Old lady he wants it bad, and your son's his kill then they have to keep him alive. I know that sounds harsh but personally I'd take it as good news."

"Christ." Jed groaned.

The sheriff turned the screen back towards himself. "Thanks Pixie for all your help. I know you have to get back. Tell your boss to call me here at the station the second he hears anything okay?"

"Sure thing Sheriff. I hope it all works out."

The sheriff shut the screen and looked at the three visibly shaken people he had in his office.

"I know I'm not going to get you to go home. The State Troopers know exactly where that van is. It won't be long before we hear something. Go back in the room and I'll come get you when I know something okay?"

Jed nodded and held the door open for Grace and Shelby. Then he followed them back to the conference room where they retook their original positions of Jed and Grace pacing and Shelby sitting with her head on her arms. They were exhausted, scared for Clay, and full of hope that he was still alive. Jed and Grace were talking quietly

Jed seemed bolstered by the news they had received. He just wanted Clay alive. His son was a tough man and knew he could handle a lot physically and emotionally. He just needed to be alive. Shelby folded her hands together and sent a prayer to God.

An hour later the Sheriff opened the door the smile on his face spoke volumes. "They got him. He's alive. A little beat up but he's alive."

"Thank Christ." Jed shuddered and Shelby saw tears rimming his eyes. Shelby sent a thank you prayer up to the heavens and hugged her Mom.

"I got him on the phone in my office. Come on." The three practically ran down the hall.

Jed took the phone from the sheriff. "Clay?" His voice broke and Shelby felt her body shake with relief.

The sheriff showed Jed the speaker

button on the phone and Jed pushed it. "Dad." Shelby wept she was so happy to hear his voice.

"Son are you alright?"

"Yea I'll be fine. I need some stitches. The fuckers taserd me that hurt like a son of a bitch."

The background noise was considerable and they had to strain to hear him. "The cops were chasing the van and when they finally forced it off the road the two guys made a run for it. The big guy, I think he's called Meat; he was killed. I can't believe this happened. I heard them talking and I think he was going to kill me to get his 1% patch."

"Yea, we heard that too. Son I am so glad you are okay. Are you coming home now?"

"Dad I can't. My bulls. I need to get back there by tonight or they can't be in the draw for the rodeo tonight."

"Son I wish I could see you."

"I know dad me too that was a close one. I'll be home in a couple weeks."

"Clay, Shelby…"

"Dad stop. I know. She's in good hands. I'll be fine." Shelby couldn't figure out why he was saying she's in good hands. Why didn't he want to talk to her? He didn't even know she was right there in the room. She wanted to grab the phone out of Jed's hands. "Listen they smashed my phone so I won't be able to talk to you. I gotta go. I have a ride to the airport. Love ya dad." Clay hung up.

Jed hung up the phone and looked to Grace then to Shelby. "Shelby I don't know what to say. I have no idea what's going on. I was going to tell him you were here but he didn't give me a chance."

"I know Jed." Shelby said quietly. "I

don't know what's going on either. The main thing is that he's okay. He's so okay he's going back to the rodeo so I'm thankful for that."

Jed nodded and Grace hugged her daughter. Shelby was stunned by what Clay said. Her mind registered that he came to New Jersey but now he acted like she was nothing to him.

They thanked the sheriff and drove home all lost in their own thoughts. The sun was still a few hours away from rising so they all went to bed to catch some much needed sleep.

Chapter 17

A few days later Liz and Lars came to visit. News had spread about Clay and his near brush with death. Liz was ecstatic that Shelby was staying in Wyoming and Lars was happy his woman was happy so their visit took on a festive nature. Shelby wished she could celebrate her new move with the same joy her friends were displaying, but inside her heart was crumbling. The only thing Shelby could think of was to why Clay hadn't contacted her yet, perhaps he couldn't handle that she was damaged goods. He didn't know she hadn't been raped, but she had been seriously violated. Maybe Clay wasn't able to handle that someone else had touched her intimately? The other scenario was that maybe Clay was mad because his ordeal all stemmed from her leaving the bar and him having to rescue her.

Shelby cried herself to sleep every night for that first week. Grace tip toed around her and tried to come up with excuses for Clays abnormal behavior. Jed was out right livid with his son. There was no way to get in touch with him and Clay obviously didn't want to talk to any because he didn't try to call anyone either.

After a week of recouping and consuming self-pity Shelby talked her Mom into allowing her to stay at her little ranch house. Shelby was going to be moving in to the house anyway, Grace just wanted to keep her close and mother her some more. Shelby was glad to be out from under her worrying Mom. She felt bad for Jed too. Grace was mad at Clay and so was his dad. Shelby knew they were having heated discussions. She didn't want to cause them any trouble; they were still newlyweds and shouldn't have to deal with her crap.

Shelby packed up and went to live in her new home. It had been two weeks now since she'd been attacked and lost Clay. She kept herself physically busy to avoid mentally breaking down. Clay hadn't tried to get in touch with her at all. He hadn't talked with anyone in the family either, so she doubted he knew she was not in Jersey anymore. Shelby approached each day like a recovering alcoholic, willing herself to just get through each day without falling to pieces. Liz and Lars visited often and even brought Mac back for another visit. They asked about Clay and Shelby told them honestly she hadn't heard from him since the attack. They were all surprised to hear that. Mac had a frown on his face. Even he didn't think it sounded like the Clay Jones he knew.

On one of the visits Liz asked Shelby if she was on Facebook. Shelby shook her head no. She never had gotten into it and then she asked Liz why. Liz looked at Lars for some confidence and then asked Shelby if she could log on to her account using her computer. Mac looked distressed and stood with his arms folded over his massive chest.

Liz logged on and summoned Shelby over. She scrolled to some photos on the screen. Shelby inhaled deeply seeing the photos. One was of Dana and Clay. Dana was hugging Clay and he stood there with his arm draped across her shoulders. Dana looked so happy she was smiling up at Clay like he was her prince. Clay wasn't smiling but he didn't look sad either. He had a half empty bottle of Jack dangling from his fingers. The next picture was Dana holding an adorable puppy. The caption under the picture was 'Look what Clay gave me.'

Shelby turned away fro the screen. "That's enough I don't want to see anymore."

"I'm sorry." Liz said as she left the chair to hug Shelby. "I just thought you should know."

"Thanks. Its better I know. It just hurts. He came to the hospital. I don't get it. Do you think he came just to break up with me?" Shelby looked to the men for answers.

Lars shrugged his shoulders and Mac actually looked pissed. The pictures sure answered a lot of questions though. He was obviously with Dana. She remembered the first night she had met Clay and how he said that giving a girl a pet was the first step in a committed relationship. Shelby sickened. She felt like such a fool.

Days passed and Shelby was slowly piecing shredded emotions back together. It had been two long and lonely weeks, but everyday she got stronger. Shelby's car and belongings arrived so she spent time personalizing her new place. She took long walks, read books she'd been meaning to read, and soaked until she was a prune in the large claw foot tub. She often got weepy thinking of how just discarded her the way he did, and then she'd pull herself together, and give herself a pep talk. She'd been hurt before by men, but this time was different. This time she felt like she trying to climb out of a muddy hole, and just when she'd get a good grip near the top, something would make her think of him, some sweet memory, and she would slide back down to the bottom of the dark hole again. She tried to justify his actions but she couldn't. She even thought that perhaps he had figured out he desired Dana and he just couldn't man up to tell her. She didn't know and perhaps that was the hardest thing she dealt with every day. She just knew she was a shell of a person trying desperately to get through each day.

Chapter 18

Clay was with everyone at the hotel bar, celebrating the rodeo's last night for a month. Everyone was in high spirits, everyone except him. Clay was broken. He had fallen so head over heels for Shelby and she'd thrown it away. He was glad she hadn't been hurt. He still didn't really know what had happened to her. His bulls had done great. Ricochet was up for rookie of the year. Dana sensed something was wrong and had tried to get Clay to talk to her. Clay didn't want to talk to anyone. She constantly hovered near him, touching him whenever she could. She was sending him a solid, undeniable message that she was there for him, but Clay continued to shrug off her affections overtures, in fact, they barely registered. He was numb.

He had been prickly as a cactus the last few weeks, but the now beers were starting to loosen him up. Dana sidled up to him and pressed her face to his chest wrapping her arm around him. Clay just looked down at her unemotionally and kept drinking his beer. A large hand clamped down on his shoulder and spun him out of Dana's arms. Mac stood in front of him, anger coursed off his large frame.

"What the fuck?" Clay said. "What are you doing here? Shouldn't you be in Jersey fucking my girl?" Even as he said it Clay felt sick.

"What?" Mac said. "You ass hole. Your girl was seriously hurt two weeks ago and you haven't even called her. But now I can see why. I really had you pegged wrong Jones."

Dana put her hands on Clays arms possessively, glaring at Mac. Clay shook her hands off his arms and growled menacingly at her.

"Damn it Dana, knock it off, I told you I'm not interested." Mac watched the exchange with interest. He turned back to Mac.

"I know she was hurt, I flew up there. You know what I found? You. I found you in her room talking about your dinner date. So don't even go there with me you shit. You need to leave. Now, because if you stay, I'm going to knock your fucking head off."

Mac stood quietly for a second.

"Are you with Dana?" Mac asked heatedly.

"No, she's my friend, that's all, and if she doesn't stop grabbing me all the time, that will even be in question." Clay looked directly at Dana when he spat out his last sentence.

Dana looked at Clay like she'd been slapped. She stomped away looking back over her shoulder and hissing out, "jerk!" to Clay.

Mac stood quietly assessing the situation.

"Clay, man we have to talk."

"There's nothing to talk about. You won. She's all yours."

"No really we need to talk, now. Are you really giving up so easily?"

Mac took Clay by the arm and Clay swung out at him clipping him on his chin. Mac stumbled backwards and glared at Clay.

"I'm going to let that go my man, but don't try it again. Clay I'm telling you. You need to hear what I have to say. It's for your benefit. Trust me."

Clay protested with a groan, and reluctantly followed Mac to a nearby table.

"Clay I'm not with Shelby and I didn't go on a date with her either. We were going to have dinner, as friends, just friends. I arrived at her apartment when those two guys that kidnapped you were attacking her. I was at the hospital because I was there initially, and I was concerned, Sara was a complete waste."

"I heard you talking Mac. I heard her tell you she wanted a rain check on your date. Your dinner date."

Mac rubbed his hand over his face. Things were beginning to make sense.

"Then did you also hear Shelby say that she would be bringing you with her?"

Clay was shocked. He hadn't heard her say that. She must have said it after he'd left.

"I didn't hear that." Clay said softly. Slowly Clay began to process what had really happened. He'd had it all wrong.

"Clay, she's really hurting, physically and emotionally. Those guys really did a number on her, seriously messed her up. Then she was damn near scared alive when you were taken. She blames herself. Then on top of everything you abandoned her when she needed you most."

"I would never leave her."

"You have left her Clay."

"I thought she didn't want me. I thought she chose you." Clay said stoically.

"Not a chance man. She made it clear from the beginning she was with you. She told Liz you either didn't want damaged goods or you were mad at her that she's the reason you had gotten into a fight with those guys which led to you being taken. She also has seen pictures on Facebook of you with Dana and the puppy you gave her. Gotta tell you I think that almost broke her."

"What? Shit." Clay said numbly. "I'm fucked. I'm gunna strangle Dana for posting those pictures. I didn't give her a puppy. I got one for Shelby. I asked Dana to watch him when I flew up there. Shit I am so fucked." He repeated.

"You probably are."

"Why didn't she tell me she was having dinner with you?'

"It was pretty last minute, she probably tried to."

Clay processed that and then looked candidly at Mac.

"Why are you here? Why are trying to help me?"

"I'm here on business. A Japanese company is investing in some cattle. They wanted to see a real rodeo. This is the last one for a while. As for helping you...Honestly I needed to know for myself if you are casting Shelby aside. If you did, if you are, then I'm going for her myself. I just couldn't believe you would toss her away like that. Clay, as much as it chaps my ass, she loves you. Well, she did love you. I care for her too. I want her to be happy."

"Oh man, I got to go see her. I have to talk to her."

"What's going on with the bulls?"

"They're already on their way back to the 5 Star. I'm flying out tomorrow."

"Come on lets get you on a plane tonight."

Clay and Mac stood up.

"Mac, I don't know what to say, thank you."

"Save it Clay. If she doesn't take you back I'm making a major play for her. She's special."

When they arrived at the airport Clay carried his duffel and the small dog carrier to the ticket counter asking for a seat on the first plane headed to Newark Airport.

"Uh-uh" said Mac. "She's in Wyoming."

Clay was visibly shaken. If she was with her Mom in Wyoming she was more hurt than he realized. Clay bought his ticket and Mac changed his open - ended itinerary so they could fly back together. Mac's car was waiting in the long - term parking lot and when they landed he drove Clay home to the 5 Star.

When Clay walked in to his house it was early morning, but still dark out. He let S'More out of his carrier to pee and then brought him inside. The rooster hadn't even stirred yet it was so early. Clay first looked in the guest room and then his room hoping to find Shelby in one of them. A shiver of despair tickled his spine. He made a pot of coffee and went to go shower. Jed heard the shower running and slammed into the bathroom.

"Clay? I'm glad to see you." Jed's eyes ran over his son's haggard appearance. The cut on his forehead stood out and Jed cringed thinking about how close he came to losing his son. He took a deep breath to compose himself. "You have some explaining to do son. We talked about this back in December. You promised me you could handle this relationship with Shelby." Jed was steamed and Clay knew Grace was probably equally upset.

"I know dad. Let me finish showering and I'll talk to you downstairs. I need a cup of coffee I've been traveling all night."

When Clay arrived down stairs still damp from his shower Jed and Grace sat side by side at the kitchen counter. Grace couldn't even look at him and his dad was holding his anger at bay with a tight- lipped frown. S'More was scampering around Grace's feet. Grace's two dogs, that she finally named Ben and Jerry, were sniffing after him while their Mom, Nellie, his Dad's dog, watched on attentively.

Clay nodded at the puppy and told them that his name was S'More and that he had picked him up a couple weeks ago to give to Shelby. He poured himself a cup of coffee and proceeded to tell them everything. He explained how after he had heard that Shelby was hurt he had gotten permission to leave his bulls. That he had hired a private plane to get to her and then about arriving at the hospital only to over hear Mac and Shelby talking about, what he thought was a date. He told them how he had known for a while that Shelby was his forever and the long distance relationship was something he wanted to change. He told them how Shelby hadn't been happy about Dana being on tour with him. That he had been keeping Dana at arms length because she had been making not so discreet overtures towards him, even though he had never given her a reason to even hope there was something more than friendship between them.

He didn't leave anything out. He then told them that Mac had been at the rodeo for business reasons and had decided to check on Clay first hand. Mac knew Clay hadn't talked to Shelby and he was concerned for Shelby's sake. Clay also told them that Mac cared for

Shelby and that if Clay didn't work things out with her that Mac was going to go above and beyond to date her. Clay then told his dad and Grace that he wasn't going to let that happen because he loved Shelby and that the last two weeks had been pure hell.

Grace started crying and Jed wrapped his arm around her. "Oh Clay she loved you so much. She got a job here to be near you. I wasn't allowed to tell you. She wanted to surprise you." Grace sniffled out. "What a mess."

Clay looked like someone had just punched him in the stomach. "You said loved." He said quietly.

"What?" Grace asked.

Clay repeated himself. "You said loved. Have I lost her?"

Grace shook her head. "I honestly don't know Clay. She thinks you're with Dana."

"Clay." His dad looked visibly relieved that

his son wasn't the uncaring moron they had been thinking he was. "You both miscommunicated. She should have told you she was going on a friend dinner date with Mac. Maybe she did, I don't know. I do know she's hurting, as are you. Think about what you're going to say to her and how you're going to say it. She needs to understand your side of it too. When she does, I think she'll forgive you. Think outside the box, son. If you love her like I think you do, you have to show her."

"Where is she?"

"She's at my, our, little ranch." Grace said as she patted Jed's arm.

Clay thought about what his dad had said. He was correct. They both had jumped to the wrong conclusions. He should have talked to her though. He shouldn't have left her hanging. He'd been so devastated that at the time, talking with her seemed like cruel and unusual punishment. He now realized he had also feared that if she did call him he wouldn't have answered because he would have thoughts that she was just calling to break up with him. He hadn't even been able to bear the idea. His jealous, stubborn, non – rational emotions had him thinking like an ostrich with its head buried in the ground, if he just avoided the issue it wouldn't hurt as badly. Unfortunately he was paying for his immaturity now.

Clay got in his truck and headed to Shelby's. Before he got to her driveway he made a U- turn and headed into town. He needed to make sure she knew he loved her. She wasn't damaged goods, he wasn't mad about the fight, he hadn't messed with Dana, and she wasn't dating Mac. It was all a big mix up, one that could have been avoided had he just walked into the hospital room.

Clay knew his entire future would be decided in the next half hour. His first goal would be to get Shelby to talk to him. According to Mac she was blaming herself for him being kidnapped. The second thing he had to rectify was that she thought he didn't want her because she had been molested by Meat and Rip, and the third and most damaging thing he prayed he could explain was that she thought he was with Dana. Two things led her to believe that; he never tried to get in touch with her after she was hurt and Dana had posted damning photos all over Facebook that Mac told him Liz had shown Shelby. Mac had showed him the pictures while they were waiting in the airport, the one of Dana holding a puppy and tagging it that Clay had given it to her, which was a total lie, could very well have sealed his fate.

It was almost noon as he turned into the drive. He had asked his Dad and Grace not to tell Shelby he was back. He didn't want her to lock him out or hide herself away at Liz's.

The newly built barn came into view first and Clay smiled seeing Grace's sheep with their lamb in the small corral nearby. As he neared the house he saw that there were two cars parked in the loop. One was Shelby's but the other he didn't recognize.

Clay got out of the truck and helped S'More down. He gathered the flowers he had bought her and headed to the front door. He rang the bell and got no answer so he then tried knocking. He couldn't hear any noise coming from inside. He realized she could be out for a walk with who ever owned the other car. Clay bent down and took the bow off from S'Mores neck. He didn't want anyone else around when he gave him to her. He placed the bow in his glove compartment of his truck and went back to the front door with S'More at his heels, and still holding the flowers.

He tried the door handle and it turned so he let himself in so he could use her phone and call her Mom to see whom she might be with. The first thing he noticed when he stepped inside was that the oven buzzer was going off and smoke was coming from within. He jogged over and quickly turned the oven off and then opened the oven door. He was yelling Shelby's name but got no answer. Thick smoke poured out causing the smoke detector to go off. Clay grabbed a dishtowel reached in and pulled out a silver pan of very burnt cookies. He tossed the entire cookie sheet including the cookies into the sink and ran water over the smoking pan sending a hiss of steam into the air.

As the smoke detector continued to beep annoyingly Clay looked around the room. Something was wrong. He felt it in every bone in his body. He saw that a glass had been over turned on the coffee table and the contents were soaking into a magazine that had been left open. Partially defrosted ice cubes lay melting in the spilled liquid.

S'More was sniffing around the patio curtains and Clay realized that the back sliding door was wide open even though the curtains were closed. He parted the thick door curtains and stepped onto the stone patio. S'More tried to follow but Clay shut the door effectively closing him inside. A red splash of color caught his eyes at the forests edge and Clay took off running towards it.

As he neared the forests he could make out two people making their way deeper into the thick trees. He could tell one of them was Shelby by her tiny stature and her athletic gait but he had no idea who the other person was. He knew something was wrong so he slowed down   enough so as to not to alert them to his presence. Carefully Clay moved, hiding his large frame behind tree after tree. He was finally close enough to see the other person clearly. It was a woman quite a bit larger than Shelby. She looked to be in her thirty's with stringy black hair. She was dressed in black jeans and a black leather vest and she had black combat boots on. She also wore a vest with a Road Tornado's Old Lady patch.

The woman was dragging Shelby into the forest yelling at her as they moved awkwardly through the dense trees. Clay noticed Shelby was wearing jean shorts, a red tee shirt and flip flops that hampered her walking. He knew this woman was forcing Shelby to walk with her but it didn't make sense. Shelby was athletic and even in her flip - flops she would have been able to out run her. It was then that Clay noticed the woman was pressing a small handgun into Shelby's side.

His throat went dry and fear snaked down his spine causing adrenaline zings to zap his fingertips. Clay squatted behind a downed log to figure out his next move. One thing he knew with certainty was that he would die before he let Shelby be hurt. He could hear the woman hurling obscenities at Shelby, which worked to his advantage allowing him to creep closer.

"My Meat is dead because of you. You whore. If you hadn't come on to him in that bar none of this would have happened!"

Shelby was cringing with the hurtful accusations. She looked frightened and Clay wished he could just snatch her away from the insane woman and comfort her.

"I didn't come on to him. I didn't. Ask Rip. They came on to me." Shelby said trying to convince the crazy lady she was innocent.

"You're as good as dead bitch. I hope the animals find your body first and then your boyfriend finds your remains. I want him to know what it's like to lose someone he loves."

It was like a cue from the heavens. Clay stepped out from behind the tree the thick branch he had found nearby tucked securely into the back waistband of his jeans.

"I do know what it's like to lose someone I love." He said. His voice was steely cold.

Both women turned towards him startled. Shelby froze as she saw Clay who was now running towards them. The larger woman aimed and fired in his direction as Shelby screamed his name. Clay dove for the ground her aim off as the bullet nicked a tree to his right. She tried to squeeze the trigger again but Shelby wacked her with her cast then pushed against her with all her might forcing her off balance. The woman cursed as she fell backwards grabbing onto Shelby's shirt pulling her down with her. Clay jumped up and ran towards them.

He saw the gun now leveled at Shelby and dove on top of the woman's arm that was holding the gun placing himself between the gun and Shelby. Shelby rolled away from them now that she was no longer being held. She heard the muffled blast from the gun as it was fired again and heard Clay grunt in pain. Icy fear sliced through Shelby and once again she called out his name. She saw him reach behind him and grab something out from behind his shirt. He raised it quickly and brought it down forcefully on the woman's head. Shelby heard the whack of the stick against her head and then saw that Meats Old lady lay motionless.

Clay rolled onto his back clutching his shoulder. A red stain bloomed on his shirt. Sweat dotted his forehead and he closed his eyes grimacing in pain. Shelby ran to him and dropped to her knees at his side.

"Clay, Clay Oh please, please, open your eyes." Shelby was pleading with him.

Clay fought the light-headedness he was experiencing and opened his eyes. Shelby was weeping over him holding her hand on his burning shoulder.

"Gun, get the gun Shel's." He managed to grunt out.

Shelby crawled over to the still unmoving woman and grabbed the gun out of her hand. She quickly crawled back to Clay.

"Clay your shot. Oh God Clay why did you do that?" Shelby was crying and scolding him.

"Baby you need to calm down. I need you. I don't have much time."

"Oh My God Clay! What!" Don't say that!"

Clay realized she thought he meant he was going to die. He actually didn't know if he was or wasn't. He was in enough pain that he very well might be ready to meet his maker, but he wasn't letting Shelby know that.

Clay was hissing the burning in his shoulder radiating down his arm. "No baby, listen. I'm losing a lot of blood. I'm going to pass out soon. I'll be okay but you're going to have to go get help. First you have to tie up the woman."

Shelby nodded quickly pulling herself together. First she took off her tee shirt leaving her in a pink lace bra. Clay looked up at her and smiled weakly.

"Are you trying to kill me woman?'

Shelby smiled back at him and said. "Don't even think about dying mister."

She gave Clay the tee shirt to hold on his wound. She then took the shoe laces from the woman's combat boots and wound the laces around her wrist that Shelby had pushed behind her. She then picked the woman up underneath her arms and dragged her to a nearby tree where Shelby propped her up. She jogged back to Clay and took off his belt. She took his belt and looped it around the laces and effectively secured Meat's Old lady to the tree with it. She then partially unlaced her other boot and looped it through the lace less boots holes thus tying her feet together. The whole process took five minutes and Shelby was drenched in sweat and breathing hard when she finished.

Shelby glanced at Clay his eyes were closed and his breathing was labored. She knew he was in pain and she could see the blood beginning to soak through her tee shirt.

"Clay, I'm going to run home and get help. I can't leave you the gun in case she wakes up and gets free and you pass out. I swear I'll run fast. Please try to stay awake. Please."

Clay nodded and Shelby stood up, flip - flops and all and took off in the fastest sprint she'd ever run.

Shelby burst through her sliding doors and almost tripped over the puppy. She didn't have time to think too much about it but it looked like Dana's pup and a stab of jealousy punched her gut knowing Clay had brought her dog with him. Shelby dialed Jed's ranch and quickly told her Mom, who answered the phone, what had happened. She told her Clay was hurt and they needed the sheriff. She explained as best she could where they were in the back forest and then hung up the phone anxious to get back to Clay. As she ran through her living room she grabbed the small quilt off the couch. She was going to use it to mark where they should enter the forest so they could be found. Shelby bolted out the sliding door making sure she shut it quickly not letting the puppy out.

Shelby dropped the quilt over a low hanging limb at the tree line and dashed back to Clay. When she arrived she noticed Clay was noticeably paler and the crazy woman was conscious. Shelby dropped down next to Clay and placed his head on her lap. She pressed the shirt against his wound causing him to groan. He didn't open his eyes.

"You're dead, you know that bitch!" The woman snarled. "You caused this. If he dies and I hope he does, it's on you!"

Shelby tried to shut out the woman's hurtful words but they were so close to the truth that they sliced through her. She was to blame. If she just hadn't run out of the bar. If she had just stayed to talk it out. Shelby stroked Clays face with her free hand.

"Whoring up to my Meat the way you did. He told me everything. You're nothing but a cock tease…"

Shelby didn't let her finish her sentence. She turned towards the woman and let lose.

"Really! You are such a fucking idiot. Do you see this gorgeous man here? Why? Why the fuck would I ever want your Meat? Why would I ever want anyone else when I had this man! Are you blind! Are you daft! Of course your boyfriend told you I came on to him! You better pray Clay doesn't die because if he does I will personally track your sorry ass down and fuck you up so bad that you'll be begging to join your loser ass hole boyfriend!"

Clay's eyes were shut but he heard every word. He was close to passing out but didn't want to leave Shelby alone. Shelby bent down and placed a gentle kiss on his brow. She sighed and a tear fell from her eyes on to his handsome face. He may not want her anymore and she knew she'd have to deal with that pain for a long time but she still loved him. God help her she still loved him.

Shelby heard a vehicle drawing closer and then she heard Jed calling her name. Shelby yelled out and kept yelling, "Over here." until Jed came into view. Her mother was right behind him. As they neared Shelby heard the wail of a siren and knew the Sheriff was also about to make an appearance.

Jed sank to his knees near his son and Shelby saw that he was shaking. "He was shot in the shoulder. I think he's passed out." Jed nodded and took over pressing the soaked tee shirt to the wound. Grace sat down next to her daughter and rubbed her back. Shelby wasn't taking her hands off of Clay. It might be the last time she ever got to touch him and the thought broke her even more.

"Mom he saved my life. She..." Shelby pointed her chin at the woman tied to the tree who was no crying. "She was going to kill me. That's Meats Old lady. Clay jumped between us and took the shot. Mom, he saved my life." Shelby's lips quivered and she began to sob into her Mom's shoulder.

The sheriff crashed through the woods

and surveyed the scene. His eyes flicked over Shelby's state of undress. He started to unbutton his shirt. "Fuck what happened? Never mind, tell me later. Clay's hurt?" He took off his Sheriff's shirt and handed it to Shelby who thanked him and pulled it on.

Jed nodded. "Shot." His voice was hard and Shelby hated how pained he sounded.

The sheriff knelt down and shook Clays unhurt shoulder. "Clay, kiddo can you hear me. Clay?" Clay's eyes fluttered open to see Shelby, his Dad, Grace and the Sheriff leaning over him. His eyes shot back to Shelby she was distraught.

"Clay we need to get you out of here. Your dad and I are going to help you but you have to try to walk. I know you're in pain son but you have to try."

Clay nodded weakly and the Sheriff and Jed gently hefted him under his shoulders.

"What about her?" Shelby said as they raised

Clay to his feet.

"I'll come back for her. Is she secure?"

"Yea, I tied her pretty good."

The small group gingerly made their way out of the forest. Jed's truck was right where Shelby had draped the quilt. They gently put Clay into the back of the king cab and Jed climbed in with him. Grace jumped into the drivers seat. Shelby jumped into the passenger seat and slammed the door. The Sheriff told them to take Clay to the town medical center. They were too far from the main hospital and he'd already lost too much blood. He told them he'd met them there after he dealt with the woman.

Chapter 19

They arrived at the medical center and Shelby jumped out and ran inside to alert the staff they had arrived. She knew the Sheriff had already called ahead for them. She dashed back outside followed by a large female nurse that was pushing a wheel chair. Jed hefted his son carefully out of the cab and placed him in the chair. Clay groaned his eyes once again fluttering open for a brief moment. The nurse wheeled Clay inside and into a back room. Jed followed but the second nurse wouldn't allow Grace or Shelby to go with them telling them there wasn't enough room for all of them.

Shelby turned to her Mom and collapsed into her arms. Grace rubbed Shelby's back trying to comfort her. "Honey he'll be okay. You did a great job."

"Mom he jumped between me and the gun. He could have been killed. I am always getting him hurt." Shelby dissolved into a fresh batch of tears. "If…if he dies…I don't think I can handle it."

Jed popped his head into the room. "The doctor is about to take the bullet out. It's not bad. He lost a lot of blood though. I need to give him some. I just wanted to tell you before we got going. He's going to be fine." Jed saw that Shelby was a mess. He quickly moved to her and pulled her into his arms.

"Shelby, honey. He'll be fine."

"Oh Jed I'm so sorry. I'm so sorry. I'm always getting him hurt. I'm so sorry." Shelby was sobbing into his shirt.

"Honey don't do this to yourself. I have to

go. He's going to be fine. I promise."

Shelby and Grace paced the waiting room and not thirty minutes later Jed reappeared. "It's over." He said pulling Grace into his arms and motioning Shelby to join them for a group hug. "He's still out but the bullets out too. The bleeding is stopped and it didn't hit anything major. He'll be as good as new in a few weeks."

"Oh Jed." Grace said. "I'm so glad. God what a day!"

Jed's voice was apprehensive and when he spoke the words came out choppily. "I'll say. This could have been bad, really bad."

The sheriff chose that moment to stride into the waiting room. He had put on another shirt. "How is he?"

"Good, he's good, thanks." Jed answered.

"Thank God." He said clapping Jed on the

shoulder. He then turned to Shelby. "Shelby I need to know what happened."

Shelby nodded and the Sheriff motioned for all of them to sit down in the plastic waiting room chairs.

Shelby began but telling them how the woman, who she learned was Meat's Old Lady, simply opened her front door and aimed a gun at her. She had been sitting on her couch with her ear buds still in since she had just finished running. Shelby said she told her who she was and that she was going to make her pay for getting her Meat killed. Shelby told them how she was forced at gunpoint to walk to the back woods. She told them how she had taken her sneakers off and put on her flip flops or she might have tried to run from her.

Grace took Shelby's hand and held it to her lips. "Oh Sweetie you could have been killed." Her Mom was shaken and Shelby grasped her hand back in a reassuring manner.

"I'm fine Mom. Clay saved me. I don't know why he was even at the house, but he was there and he saved my life."

Shelby then went on to explain how Clay had somehow found them and what transpired after that.

Jed and Grace looked at each other sending a silent message to each other. The sheriff stood up. "Well I got everything I need. Shelby I'll need you to come to the station tomorrow and fill out a formal report okay."

"Sure Sheriff I'll come down. I'll bring your shirt back too." Shelby smiled at him try to convey her thanks but the smile didn't reach her eyes. They stood up and thanked him before he left.

The nurse came out and told the three of them that Clay was awake. Jed left Grace and Shelby giving them each a hug and went to see his son. He was only gone for a few minutes when he reappeared and nodded to Shelby.

"He's still a little groggy but he wants to see you."

Shelby looked frightened and glanced quickly at her mother who encouraged her by saying. "It will be alright honey. Go see him."

Shelby walked through the door that Jed was now standing by and looked up at him as she passed by. She stopped and turned around and stepped back towards Jed. "Jed, I need to tell you. I mean…I need you to know, that I would never, ever, purposely place Clay in danger." Shelby's eyes were filled with tears again her chin quivered as she tried not to break down completely.

Jed reached out and placed his hand on her shoulder in a fatherly manner.

"Sweetheart I know that. Clay knows that too, don't worry."

Shelby nodded acknowledging his acceptance of her statement. She sniffed and wiped her eyes with the sheriff's shirtsleeve.

Shelby turned and headed down the sterile hallway. At the third door she saw Clay lying on a bed with his shirt off and his shoulder bandaged. The sheets on the bed were pulled to his waist and Shelby sucked in a sharp upon seeing his beautifully sculpted chest for the first time in many long months. The man was rock hard in all the right places. As Shelby entered the room Clay opened his eyes and gave her a small smile. She walked to the bed's edge and looked down at the man who had sent her world spinning out of control and was now, probably about to hurl it into Never - Never land.

"Hi." She said quietly. She had to fist her hand tightly on the hospital bed rail to stop herself from reaching out and touching his handsome face.

"Hi." He repeated back to her. "Are you okay?"

"Clay, don't you think that's my line?" She teased him softly.

"No baby it's my line."

Shelby lowered her gaze to rest on her hand that was gripping the bed rail.

"Clay you saved my life. I still can't believe you dove on the gun like that. You're nuts." Her voice was soft and her sad smile squeezed his heart.

"No, I knew exactly what I was doing." They were both quiet for a few ominous seconds.

"Shelby I need to talk to you. The doctor said I can leave in a few hours and when I do can I please come to your house so we can talk?"

"It's okay Clay, I know. You don't have to come over."

"Shel's you don't know. Please say you will wait at home for me so we can talk. It would mean a great deal to me."

Shelby sent him a lopsided smile. "Well since you asked so nicely and since you did just save my life… Yes, I'll be home so we can talk." Shelby saw Clay close his eyes still in obvious discomfort but now his lips were slightly turned up in a very small smile.

"Clay?"

"Ummm?"

"If you decide not to come over. If you decide we don't need to talk. Would you please call me and let me know?" Clay opened his eyes and found hers. He wished he could hold her. He may have been in pain from the bullet but she was also hurting and he knew he was the cause of it.

"I'll be over Shelby." Clays said sleepily as his eyes started to close again. Shelby watched with a heavy heart as the post operation pain medicine claimed him. She lingered at his bedside and without thought brushed the hair back from his brow and placed a tender kiss on his cheek. Her eyes filled again while looking at him. She knew tonight's talk would be one of the hardest things she would ever have to endure, but she vowed she's do it. She'd be strong for Clay. She remembered the advice she had given Liz once.

'If you love something set it free.

If it comes back to you it's yours forever.

If it doesn't it was never yours to begin with.'

How appropriate that saying was now Shelby thought.

Chapter 20

Grace drove Shelby back to the little ranch. They had left Jed to wait on Clay to wake enough to go home. Grace was going back to pick them up when Jed called. They hadn't spoken on the ride home and Shelby was grateful for the quiet. She didn't want her Mom to know how much she was hurting. Shelby noticed that Meat's Old Ladies car was gone. The sheriff had said he was having it towed. She was grateful Rosie had removed it so quickly. When the truck pulled to a stop Shelby gave her Mom a swift peck on her cheek thanking her and then she quickly got out of the truck hoping to thwart any motherly advice. She reached her front steps, her Mom, being a Mom, was waiting for her to get inside safely.

When Shelby opened her front door the little ball of fur sprinted past her yapping excitedly to be free from the confines of the house.

"Oh Gosh." Shelby said. "I forgot about you. Mom!"

Grace watched Shelby pick up S'More and walk him to the truck. "Mom you have to take Dana's dog back to Clay." Shelby deposited S'More in the back of the cab.

"Shelby…" Grace started to say something and then thought better of it. "Okay sweetie. Call me if you need anything."

"Thanks Mom I'll be fine. Love you."

"Love you too honey."

Shelby walked inside her home her heart was crumbling. She needed to steel herself for the conversation she knew was coming in a few short hours.

It was closing in on dusk when Clay turned down her driveway. He hoped he had everything he needed for the second time that day. He had made his Dad go buy more flowers and he had reattached the bow around S'Mores little neck. He pulled around the loop of the small ranch and got out of his truck holding the flowers and a wiggly S'More. Clay rang her doorbell and heard feet shuffling around inside. He was nervous. She had said she would talk to him, but he couldn't help but worry that if there was too much damage done, he will have lost her.

Shelby opened the door to find Clay holding Dana's puppy and a beautiful bouquet of flowers. Clay's hand was gently wrapped around the little puppy as it tried to squirm free from his arms.

Shelby had to steady herself using the doorframe. The bastard brought his girlfriends dog with him to break up with me, this sucks, she thought grimly. Her eyes locked on the puppy and then she closed her eyes in order to compose herself.

"Shelby? What's the matter? You said we could talk." Clay said noticing her bleak expression.

Shelby didn't respond. She was weak kneed at seeing him standing in front of her. She remembered how he had looked just a few hours earlier when he was laying bloodied and in pain in the woods. Her emotions were threatening to tumble out unchecked. She had to stay in control. She saw the puppy was slipping out of Clays grasp and watched him put him down.

Shelby hung her head and looked at the floor. She couldn't keep doing this with him. He was physically and emotionally hurting her, she needed to move on, she needed closure.

"You could have cleared things with me over the phone Clay. I don't need the peace offering." She said looking at the flowers. "And for the record; bringing your girlfriend's dog with you to make nice with your old girlfriend…well that's boarder line mean." Shelby voice was so hushed he barely made out what she said. He saw her chin quivering as she tried not to cry.

Clay reached for the doorframe to steady himself. He was so mad. Shelby leaned away from his hand and he cringed that she had moved away from him. "Shelby stop, just stop. Dana is not my girlfriend!" His voice was hard, she could tell he was angry.

"Clay…" Shelby was losing the emotional battle and tears started running down her face.

Clay regained his composure with a calming breath. Shelby saw the scar marring his forehead from when he'd been kidnapped and how he moved his body so he wouldn't jar his shoulder. She let out a breath she didn't even know she'd been holding.

"We need to talk Shelby. You're right about one thing; we do need to clear things up. I need to tell you what happened and you need to listen."

Shelby stepped aside and Clay walked her to the couch, motioning for her to sit. He sat opposite her on the coffee table so he could face her. The puppy was sniffing everywhere and Shelby's eyes followed the cute little thing as it explored the room. She wanted to look anywhere but at Clay. Clay put the flowers on the floor near his cowboy boots and took Shelby's hands in his. She pulled them back and held them tightly together in her lap.

"Shelby when I heard you were hurt I jumped through hoops to get to you. I had to go to the PBR board so I could leave my bulls. I chartered a private plane. I was so worried about you. I had no idea what happened. Actually I still don't. I just knew I had to get to you."

Clay paused and took a steadying breath. His voice was choppy with emotion. "When I got to the hospital I heard you talking with Mac about a ruined dinner date. I thought you were dating Mac. I was shocked Shelby. I was so angry I don't even remember walking out of the hospital."

Shelby looked at him and crumbled as tears rained down her cheeks. She couldn't believe the terrible timing of it all. Clay had come for her. He hadn't come to break up with her.

"Oh God, It wasn't a date. It was nothing. I knew you came to the hospital, but I thought you were taken before you had a chance to come in. Then after you were rescued and you didn't want to talk to me...I just thought you were there to break up with me."

"No baby I came for you." Clay quickly interjected.

Shelby drew in an unsteady breath. "I just couldn't understand what had changed.

What I had done to cause you to not want me any more. It was awful. When I saw the Facebook pictures, well then I knew she had won you back." Shelby's body rocked back and forth as the painful memories pored out of her.

"I didn't even know about the pictures Shelby. I was never with Dana, not even after I thought you were with Mac."

"But the puppy?"

"I never gave her a puppy, Shel's."

Shelby looked back to the cute little ball of fur chewing on a corner of the rug.

"I was standing outside of your hospital room. I didn't come in at first, because I thought you were with a doctor and I didn't want to barge in if you were being examined. Then I recognized Mac's voice."

Shelby's body stilled and her fist pressed heavily against her heart, as she comprehended the enormity of what Clay had over heard. She instantly empathized with him knowing if the roles had been reversed she too would have acted similarly. In fact hadn't she refused to talk to Clay for three long days just because he had helped a drunk Dana back to her hotel room?

Clay had paused to get his train wreck of emotions under control. "I heard you tell him you needed a rain check on your dinner date. It crushed me, Shelby. Here I'd been doing everything I could to keep my distance from Dana because I didn't want you upset. I tried so hard to make sure you understood how I felt about you. How much I loved you. Then I hear you talking about dating Mac. I left. I couldn't handle seeing you with him. I was broken."

"I would never do that Clay. You could have given me the chance to explain Clay."

"You could have told me you were meeting with him." He countered.

"It was so spur of the moment. I was going to

tell you. I wasn't trying to hide it. I was just afraid you might misconstrue that it wasn't a date."

"Too late baby." Clay bit out. "I wish like hell I had come into that room now, but I was so mad at you. I was hurting."

"I was hurting Clay." Shelby's voice rose. "I was assaulted. Those men did terrible things to me. All I wanted was you. I kept hoping you would call me. I needed you Clay. I really needed you. So many scenarios as to why you didn't want to talk to me kept running through my mind. I thought you wanted Dana, or maybe you didn't like that I was molested. Then you were kidnapped and I thought you were mad that I was the reason you were targeted because you fought those men when I ran from the bar. Clay those hours you were gone, when they had you; I didn't know if you were dead or alive, it was my worst nightmare. We were a mess. Your Dad, my Mom, me, we were so worried." Shelby was fighting back more tears.

"Shelby this is such a cluster fuck. I thought you didn't want us…want more."

"What a mess." Shelby put her face in her hands and started sobbing uncontrollably.

Clay moved off the table and knelt before her pulling her into his arms. Shelby buried her head in the crook of his neck.

"We are fixing this sweetheart. I told you before I will never not want you."

"Maybe you should know what happened to me before you say that."

"It's not going to matter. I love you. I want to hear about it. I need you to tell me and I want you to see that no matter what, you are still my girl."

Shelby's head was spinning. He still loved her. She was still his girl. The crushing weight that had been fisting her chest was beginning to loosen.

Clay moved so he was sitting next to

Shelby on the couch. He gently lifted her even though it hurt his shoulder and arranged her so she was cradled on his lap. He needed the physical contact like he needed air. Her head was resting against his good shoulder. She didn't resist their closeness, which Clay took as a good sign, but her hands returned to her lap holding them in tight white knuckled fists. He knew she was anxious to tell him the details involving the assault.

"Tell me what happened baby, tell me everything, I want to know. I need to know. I need to take some of this pain from you."

Shelby took a deep breath and wiped her tears with the back of her hand. Clay helped her by wiping his shirtsleeve on her cheeks then tenderly using it to wipe her nose. He steeled himself for what she was going to tell him. He needed to be strong for her.

Shelby told Clay everything that she remembered. She then told Clay what Mac had told her about what she didn't remember.

Clay didn't utter a word. She could feel the anger emanating off him as his arms holding her turned to steel. She knew his anger was directed at Meat and Rip, not her. She told Clay every sordid detail; she didn't leave anything out. When she finished she looked up into Clays face and sighed. Just telling him made her feel better. Clay now knew more than anyone, more than Mac, the police, and even her Mom. Clay tilted her chin up with a crooked finger so she was looking into his eyes. Tears slid quietly down his face.

"I'm so sorry baby. I'm so sorry you were hurt. I'm so sorry I left without checking on you. I can't undo these last two weeks. I wish I could, but I can't. I'm just thankful you're alive. I'm so grateful that Mac got there when he did."

Shelby wiped Clays tears off his cheeks. Her big, bad - ass cowboy was crying for her and her heart melted. "I'm sorry I didn't tell you about Mac right away. I didn't want you to get upset. I didn't want to open the door for you to have dinner with Dana. I know that was selfish. I'm so sorry."

"I'm going to tell you something that might not be in my best interest right now, but I want you to know. I want our slate completely clear." Shelby cocked her head and looked up at him wondering what he could possibly say. Clay took a deep breath. "Mac really cares for you. He wants more than friends with you. If you feel the same way about him, I'll step aside, but it would kill me."

Shelby lifted her arms and put her hands behind Clays neck stroking her fingers through his hair. Her cast rubbed on Clays skin but he wasn't going to tell her that. He wanted her to touch him.

"No I care about Mac as a friend, that's all. I needed you Clay. You were the only one I wanted to talk to after it happened. I've never felt so lost."

"I'm here now. I won't leave unless you tell me too."

Shelby leaned her head against his chest. Clay had his arms wrapped around her and his chin rested on top of her head. They sat like that for a long time, neither wanting to separate.

Clay planted a kiss on Shelby's forehead. He was nervous she hadn't answered him.

"I don't want you to leave Clay. I've missed you. I've missed us."

His relief was so tangible Shelby felt the moment his body relaxed. "Shelby I never stopped loving you. I love you so much. I missed us too."

She sighed but it sounded like a little whimper. She was so relieved, the tension draining out of her. Clay held her tightly to him.

Shelby nodded into his shirt. "I still love you too, Clay. I've ached without you."

Clay stroked her back with his hand. "Can we get past this, Shel's?"

"I'd like to Clay. It has been an awful couple of weeks. I know this was partly my fault too. I'm sorry you thought I was with Mac."

"These have been some of the worst weeks of my life, Shelby. I barely talked to anyone. I didn't want to call home because I didn't want my Dad or your Mom to even say your name."

"They are going to be so happy. Do they know? I mean that you still like me?"

"Love you Shels and yes, I flew in early this morning with Mac …"

"Mac?" Shelby interrupted.

"Yea, it's a long story, but I owe him big time."

"If he brought you back to me then I owe him too."

"This morning when I came over it was to

talk to you, to have this talk we are having now. When I saw you being hauled into the woods with that gun pressed into your side I was so afraid Shel's. I was afraid I'd never get the chance to fix us. To let you know that I have always loved you."

"Clay…" Shelby buried her head into his shirt and breathed in his masculine scent. God she even missed how he smelled.

"Shel's you have no idea how much I've missed you. I never want to lose you again. I know it's cliché but you do complete me. Nothing was important without you to share it with me."

Shelby hugged Clay tighter as the nightmare of the past weeks began to recede like a balloon losing air. A shuffling noise drew Shelby's eyes to the small bundle of fur poking around her firewood bin.

"Ummm, so Clay is that your puppy? And who put that blue bow around its neck?"

Clay lifted Shelby up and placed her back on the couch. He went to the puppy scooping him up in his strong arms and placed him gently on Shelby's lap.

"This is S'More's. I bought him for you back before all this crap even happened. I asked Dana to watch him when I flew to New Jersey. That's when she took that damn picture."

"S'More?"

"Yup he has the colorings of a S'More, graham cracker brown, chocolate brown and marsh mellow white, but personally I like the play on words. S'More…More. Get it?" Clay sent her mischievous smile.

Clay knelt down on one knee in front of Shelby while keeping his hand on the fidgeting pup so he couldn't run away. Shelby went to pet S'More and noticed something hanging from the ribbon tied around his neck. She looked closer then gasped. A beautiful diamond ring was threaded though the ribbon.

Shelby looked at Clay who was still perched on one knee in front of her. Her heart was thumping madly. Clay was looking into her eyes with unchecked emotion.

"Shelby Jensen. I love you. I don't want to waste anymore time not being with you. I want to fall asleep holding with you, wake up next to you, take walks with you, and eat every meal with you. I want to dance with you at Bennett's every Saturday night and I don't want to share. I want children with you. I want to provide for you, share everything with you. Build a life with you. I want more with you, Shelby. I want a chance for more. Will you marry me?"

Shelby was speechless. S'More was trampling her lap wearing a beautiful diamond ring and the man of her dreams just proposed to her.

Clay stayed on his bended knees awaiting her answer. He was so nervous that sweat tickled his brow. His grandpa had once told him, "Go big or go home." Clay decided to go big. He figured if she couldn't forgive him then he was going to continue to fight for her and if she did forgive him he wasn't wasting anymore time. He wanted her forever and she needed to know that.

Shelby saw the man that she knew she couldn't live without in front of her. She remembered back to the first time she saw him. This man completed her too. He knew her so well. Sometimes better than she knew herself. She knew she loved him. As corny as it sounded she knew he was her soul mate. He was her chance for more.

"Yes Clay. Yes I'll marry you."

Clay jumped up and grabbed her off the couch so he could hug her. Shelby was giggling with his antics. He suddenly released her and Shelby watched him race after S'More who had scampered off into the kitchen.

Clay's returned holding S'More and with shaky hands untied the ribbon from the puppy's neck. He put S'More down and dangled the ribbon over his hand so the ring fell into his palm. He took the ring and slid it on to Shelby's left hand ring finger, and then he sealed it there with a kiss. The ring was magnificent. It was a round cut diamond with sapphires surrounding the main stone. The diamonds and sapphires continued down the sides adorning the platinum band.

"Clay it's beautiful. I love it. I love you. Thank you."

"You're beautiful and thank you for agreeing to be my wife."

S'More chose that moment to knock something over in the kitchen. "We can keep him right?" He asked Shelby sheepishly.

"Of course!" Shelby's thoughts turned back to one of their first conversations regarding men giving pets to woman. She was grinning from ear to ear.

"I know what you're remembering baby. The first day we met. I remember that conversation we had in the barn about a guy giving a girl a pet. That was my initial game plan. It was going to be my pre-courting gift." Clay said as he stroked her cheek with his hand.

"Let's take him outside, okay?"

Shelby bent down and picked up the beautiful flowers Clay had brought. She took them in the kitchen and placed them in a vase before joining Clay who was sitting on the front steps as S'More frolicked in the nearby grass.

"So you know I've moved here I guess?" She said with a laugh.

"Your mom told me this morning. You got the job I circled in the paper?"

"Yes, thank you. That gesture; leaving me

the classifieds and circling the job, knowing if I got it I'd have to move here, Clay, that's when I knew."

"Knew what honey?"

"Knew how you really felt about me."

Clay looked over at her raising an eyebrow.

"Shel's I'd already told you I loved you."

"I know, but actions speak louder than words. That showed me."

Clay put his arm around her and she gladly leaned in to him.

"Want to go tell our parents?" Shelby said.

"I do. I just don't want to share you yet." Clay rested his head on top of hers.

Epilogue

During the first week of their engagement Clays bulls arrived back on the 5 Star and Clay stayed busy with them and all the other daily chores he tended to on the ranch. An inspector from the PBR was due to show up in the next few weeks and Clay needed to make sure his stock were in prime condition, he didn't want to lose his contract.

During week two of their engagement their parents had taken them to dinner and told them that they wanted to move into Grace's house on the little ranch, where Shelby and Clay were currently residing. They thought Shelby and Clay should live on the 5 Star. Clay had taken over most of the day-to-day operations at the ranch. He had made lucrative connections on the PBR circuit and now the 5 Star had beef supply contracts with two more restaurants and a grocery store chain. Clay was proving himself to be a good businessman. Shelby was infinitely proud of him. It made sense for Clay to live on the ranch. Jed told them he wanted to stay involved with the ranch, but scaled down. He wanted to enjoy his beautiful new wife and maybe even travel a little. Jed had also told them he had retired from coaching. There was no way he was leaving Grace for any extended period of time.

Shelby and Clay were floored that they were going to be living at The 5 Star. They both loved the big ranch. Shelby was nervous, but finally asked if she could, rearrange furniture, take down or put up different pictures, basically put her personal touch on the house. Jed didn't even hesitate when he answered. He told her and Clay that the house was theirs. He and Clay would go over the logistics at another time and they would include their wives in that conversation, but the bottom line, the 5 Star was going to support both households. So the week before Clay and Shelby were to marry she and her Mom were in switch residence mode.

Shelby and Clay hadn't wanted a big fancy wedding. They just wanted to be married. Shelby's Mom and Clay's dad talked them out of eloping that first night when they had told them they were back together and getting married. Grace and Jed were adamant about wanting to be with them when they tied the knot, and they wanted their friends there also. Reluctantly Clay and Shelby decided to wait two weeks to allow for her mom and his dad to plan and organize their wedding. Shelby and Clay let them take the reigns and they happily organized everything.

On their wedding day Shelby and Clay

basked in the support and love of their family and friends. Sara and Danny had flown in. A few of Shelby's and her Mom's friends flew west for the nuptials. Many of Jed's friends and town's people were in attendance as well. They had watched Jed raise Clay alone and they loved Clay like he was their own son. Clay's friends from town and State came to wish them well. Many outwardly thanking Shelby for taking him off the market, hoping now the girls would now pay attention to them. Dana and her family attended. Shelby accepted her well wishes and only cringed a little when she hugged her husband. The Dade family attended, along with Lars and Mac. Clay knew Mac had saved their relationship and he thanked him by giving him all the 5 Star lawyer business, which was turning out to be substantial.

The only blip on the day was when Clay's Mom, Mona, tried to sit by Jed in the church. Clay left his place at the alter, where he had been standing waiting somewhat impatiently for his bride to appear, and whispered discreetly in his mother's ear. Much to everyone's surprise Mona got up and moved to sit in the second row without causing a scene. Jed sent Clay a silent thank you.

The church service was short but poignant each repeating their own written vows. The reception was back at the 5 Star. It had been decorated professionally and lights twinkled from all the trees and the tables held beautiful vases of colorful wildflowers. The meal was catered by Busters and was delicious. A 6-piece band played a variety of music that kept many people, young and old alike running to the dance floor. Everyone was having a great time. Clay held Shelby close as they swayed to the music on the wooden floor that had been brought in for the wedding. Their love was palatable to anyone watching them. They were always touching each other, always stealing little kisses and those few minutes they were apart they found each other with their eyes.

Clay pointed out S'More to Shelby as they watched him career around the barn chasing the other dogs. And they both laughed.

"You know what's next Shel's?" He whispered softly in his bride's ear.

Shelby looked up at her handsome husband and smiled. "Does it have anything to do with giving S'More a brother or sister?"

"Yes baby and I am not talking about a furry sibling either." He said nuzzling her neck. Shelby giggled with his tender touch.

"I love you Shel's. I knew it the second I saw you. You know I saw a picture of you on your Mom's phone before I even had met you. God I just knew even then you were special."

"I love you too Clay. I knew I was in trouble Christmas day."

"Trouble?"

"Good trouble Honey. The kind I always want to be in." She smiled saucily up at him.

Shelby snuggled closer into Clays arms. "I love our 'more' Shels."

"Me too Clay. Me too."

ABOUT THE AUTHOR

Zanne Sweeney is a graduate from Kent State University. She is a teacher, and coach, who loves to write stories that she hopes her readers won't want to put down. "That's the ultimate compliment."

When she's not teaching, coaching, or writing Zanne loves to spend time with her family and fun loving friends. She is a novice photographer, is a consummate sports fan, and never without a book to read.

You can reach out to Zanne on Twitter @zanneweeney and on her Facebook like page: Zanne Sweeney - Author. https://www.facebook.com/zanne.sweeney.author?ref=hl